WOLVES OF THE
BEYOND

SPIRIT WOLF

KATHRYN LASKY

WOLVES OF THE BEYOND

SPIRIT WOLF

SCHOLASTIC PRESS / NEW YORK

ISBN 978-0-545-48789-4

10 9 8 7 6 5 4 3 2 1   12 13 14 15 16

Printed in the U.S.A.   40
This edition first printing, September 2012

Map illustration by Lillie Howard
Book design by Lillie Howard

The darkness drops again; but now I know
That twenty centuries of stony sleep
Were vexed to nightmare by a rocking cradle,
And what rough beast, its hour come round at last,
Slouches towards Bethlehem to be born?

William Butler Yeats, "The Second Coming"

CONTENTS

Dream Shards 1

1 A Scarlet Rain..5

2 Castaways 13

3 A Strange Voice 19

4 A Tail Reclaimed 21

5 Water Wing..34

6 Another Pelt 45

7 Out of Chaos 52

8 The Broken Ring...59

9 The Cairn of the Fengos 65

10 Almost as Good as Two Eyes............................75

11 Shattered 81

12 The Offing 89

13 "No! No, and No Again!"....................................94

14 Beyond the Beyond, Before the Before 99

15 The Long Blue Night 107

16 Of Wolves and Metal 115

17 The New Great Chain 121

18 Blood and Stars 125

19 The Toe of the Glacier.............................132

20 Into the Spirit Woods 137

21 The Wind of Her Wings 145

22 Bits of Miracles....................................154

23 Bronka 161

24 This View of Life!................................170

25 "He Still Lives".....................................182

26 The Moon Crack...................................189

27 The Loveliest of Bones.........................198

28 "Who Is This?" 203

29 The Crystal Plain 205

30 A Wolf Named Aliac 215

31 Caila!...220

32 The Last Den..224

DREAM SHARDS

THE SILVER WOLF STOOD UP IN the cave where he had been sleeping. Something had woken him. He was not sure what — a slight tremor in the floor of the cave? He shook his head as if to clear it. He had been dreaming something important, but he could make no sense of it. The dream had fractured and its shards were now scattered around him. He could only feel pieces of it, but they drew him closer to the very heart of a secret, a secret deep within his soul, that had long perplexed him and haunted his sleep.

He put his nose close to the ground as if he might be able to track the scent of these shards. He knew it was stupid, but he couldn't fight the compulsion. In the dream there was a pelt, silver like his own, but tattered, raggedy, like that of a very old wolf. He had thought of it as a first

1

pelt, whatever that meant. How many pelts could one wolf have? But the words "first pelt" rattled in his marrow. Faolan's anxiety increased as he paced the tight space of the cave. He shut his eyes to concentrate and a dim memory of a very old, very frail wolf came back to him. He began scraping the ground hard with his misshapen paw as if to dig deeper into the secrets. Was the wolf some sort of messenger? Words from the dream began to stream through his head. *My service is not over. I am in but my first pelt of a new season. Can this be so?*

Faolan stepped toward the cave opening and saw his two sisters limned in the light of a full moon. They were diligently gnawing the bones of their mother, Morag, in order to honor her. When they were finished, they would place the bones with others that Faolan had carved on a cairn, a *drumlyn*, on this lonely prospect of Broken Talon Point. Faolan had selected this specific place because on a clear night he would be able to see the *drumlyn* from his watch at the Ring of Sacred Volcanoes. And from here, on this peninsula of land that hooked out into the Sea of Hoolemere like the broken claw of an owl, he could see the jagged ring of flames that shot from the volcanoes.

Tonight every volcano was active, so the five crowns appeared like a circle of glowing rubies against a sky roiling with silver-lit clouds. The snow of Broken Talon Point had been scoured by the sea winds, leaving a sheath of ice. As Faolan stepped from the cave, he felt something shiver beneath his paws. The ice began to splinter. Beezar, the small constellation known as the blind wolf that stumbled across the night, gave a great lurch and seemed to crash. The stars shuddered and the sky began to slide as the earth convulsed. Mhairie and Dearlea stood locked with fear. There was a deep rumbling that burst from the very center of the earth and then a shattering crack that threw the two sisters onto their backs.

They scrambled to their feet again but the earth was still shaking too violently. They tried to wrap their paws and legs around each other, clinging to each other as they looked toward the sky.

"Look! Look!" Mhairie gasped, her eyes wide with terror. Flames swept through the night.

"It's the Ring!" Dearlea cried. One by one, like stars dying, the volcanoes collapsed into themselves, shooting rivers of flame and smoke into the sky.

"What's happening?" Dearlea shrieked. "Look to the east!" But once again the earth was seized with a deep and terrible spasm. A huge rock shot straight up into the air, almost crushing Faolan as it crashed to the ground.

Then there was a new sound. A jagged, tearing noise from the north. The three wolves wheeled about and caught sight of a white tide of ice advancing toward them, the leading edge jagged with frozen fangs. The H'rathghar glacier, anchored for centuries, had cut loose and was plowing across the open water. They felt another tremendous quaking beneath their paws and were thrown down again onto the frozen ground. It was as if the center of the earth could not hold.

On his back, Faolan saw the moon throbbing in the flame-ripped night. He began slipping on the ice and clawed feebly at the sky as if to gain purchase. Beneath him he felt the spasms of the dying earth. *I am rocking in the cradle of my lost souls*, he thought. The constellation of the Great Bear blazed above him, and Lupus and Skaarsgard had suddenly reappeared, in defiance of the season.

The earth had slipped its moorings and the constellations hung haphazardly in the sky without rhyme or reason.

His sisters screamed and Faolan whipped his head around to see the peninsula fracture. The two she-wolves scrambled and struggled, but slid inexorably off the edge into the sea. The last thing Faolan saw was Dearlea's bright green eyes roll back into her head until they showed only white — the white of the glacier's fangs that tore across that sea.

CHAPTER ONE

A Scarlet Rain

THAT SAME EVENING AT THE Ring of Sacred Volcanoes, Edme had just finished her watch and was descending from the volcano Morgan. The shift had been tinged with unbearable sadness, as had the last several. For more than twelve moons, the wolves had endured the most desperate of times in the long history of the Beyond. Their prime source of meat, the caribou herds, had disappeared. Famine had set in. It was a period of endless hunger moons, for springs and summers seemed to have vanished along with the herds, leaving only ice. So many wolves had died, and if that were not bad enough, a false prophet had emerged in the midst of the chaos. He wore the mask and helm of a heroic warrior owl, Gwyndor, and under the guise of helping the starving wolves, had instead led many to their death.

Together Faolan and Edme had helped capture the Prophet, but the damage he caused could not be undone. And in the meantime, Faolan had taken his sisters to the *drumlyn* of their mother, so that the three of them could pay homage to her. This had left Edme alone, away from her closest friends. She missed them all and of course she missed those who were gone forever, those who had died in the famine. First there had been the death of her dear *taiga*, Winks, and her friend Tearlach. Now with Faolan and his sisters gone, Edme felt utterly bereft. She was alone, so alone.

By the time she was at the base of the cairn where she had stood watch, tears had begun to spill from Edme's single eye. Then there was a deep rumble from the volcanoes, and a tall slim flame scratched at the sky. It was an unusually deep bloodred color. Edme's tears caught the reflection of the flame just as Twist was passing by. He stopped in his tracks.

"I say! Are you all right, Edme? Have you been cut?"

"What? What are you talking about?" Edme asked.

"Oh," said Twist. "For a second, I thought there was blood coming from your eye, Edme. But I see it was just the light. Ha! Silly old me."

He turned his head toward the H'rathghar volcano. "I tell you, the old girl's been acting up a bit lately. They all have — all five of them." He paused. "Gone a bit peculiar. Well" — he turned back to the path — "these are peculiar times, my dear. Had a good watch, I take it?"

"Oh, yes. A fine watch."

There was a terrific cracking sound and Edme saw Twist stagger. The ground beneath their paws ruptured and Twist vanished before her eyes. Another jolt rocked her, and she felt a hot gust that sucked her straight up into the air. The world turned black and there was a rain of red embers.

The Ring is collapsing. The ember is no more. My service is over, I am free, soon to die alone. Alone, alone!

These were the last thoughts to rake through her consciousness, then all went black.

Far from the Ring, in the Shadow Forest above a blue spruce tree, the Masked Owl Gwynneth floated in the smooth velvet air of the night. The tree was the site of her father, Gwyndor's, grave and hero mark, which had finally been restored after it was desecrated by the Prophet. In a high hollow in the tree, his bones and his mask rested — peaceful at last after the despicable treachery of Liam MacDuncan. The MacDuncan chieftain had stolen Gwyndor's mask to disguise his identity as he led the starving wolves of the Beyond to their destruction. A "prophet" he had called himself. The very idea of his using her father's mask for such vile deception made Gwynneth want to yarp up a pellet. But now that the hero mark had been restored, it was time for her to seek peace.

Splendid, splendid, the voice that was not quite a voice whispered as Gwynneth placed the last bone in the hollow. A scroom appeared as a vaporous mist, floating down through the branches of the tree.

On the ground below Gwynneth, the Sark tipped up her muzzle. "Do you smell that? No, of course you don't. Owls can't smell worth a pile of caribou scat."

"I smell it," Liam MacDuncan said. He seemed to have sunken into a permanent posture of submission. His tail was tucked so firmly between his legs that he might have been without one entirely, tailless.

Suddenly, a gust of wind blew the scroom apart and the spruce began to shake.

The tiny vertebrae that Gwynneth had just placed so carefully in the tree's hollow flew out like white hailstones.

"Great Glaux!" Gwynneth shreed in the earsplitting screech of a Masked Owl. She looked below and saw the

Sark stagger. A boulder from an escarpment tumbled down the hill and Liam MacDuncan gave an agonized howl as his bones crunched under the weight of the rock.

"Run, Sark, run!" But when Gwynneth looked down, she couldn't see the Sark anywhere. Below was a scene of utter devastation. Great gouges scored the thick blanket of snow that had so long covered the Beyond and the Shadow Forest. Trees had toppled, and the blue spruce tilted at an alarming angle, casting vertebrae out from the hollow, though Gwyndor's mask remained firmly lodged.

"This is where the mask belongs, whatever happens," Gwynneth whispered to herself. This was her father's hero mark.

The air around her once again began to shiver. The trees began to twitch in some sort of antic dance and Gwynneth, hovering above it all, saw the roots of this ancient forest begin to pop from the ground. She felt her wings seizing up. *Glaux, I am going yeep!*

Fear had stalled her gizzard and the instinct to fly deserted her. She heard the deafening *crack* of the blue spruce as it crashed down in the scalding moonlight, streaked with fiery traces of volcanic embers. Her father's helm twirled down, down, slowly down, as if a red devil owl were spinning through the night. Gwynneth's wings locked against her sides and she hurtled toward the ground.

The Whistler, a painfully thin wolf assigned to the Blood Watch far to the west of the Ring of Sacred Volcanoes, had taken to sleeping in the strange cave that Faolan had shown him more than a moon ago. It was a peculiar place with odd drawings on many of the walls, passages, and underground tunnels, but it reminded him of his best friend, Faolan.

The Whistler had met Faolan when Faolan had rejoined the MacDuncan clan after almost a year as a lone wolf. The Whistler and Faolan were both gnaw wolves, having been cursed at birth with some sort of deformity. They were called *malcadhs*, a word that meant "cursed" in the language of the wolves. The Whistler's curse was almost invisible until he opened his mouth to growl or speak and revealed his twisted windpipe. There was a jagged hole in it that made his spoken words sound like a shrill whistling hiss. Some young pups delighted in calling him "Snake," because of the hissing, but all that taunting had disappeared in the time of the famine. No one had the energy for bullying and abuse when the hunger moons had continued unendingly and the wolves were starving.

In the past month, the Whistler had been assigned a post that would once have been unthinkable for a gnaw wolf. He was a member of the Blood Watch that guarded the border between the Beyond and the Outermost, where the savage outclanners lived. Now, no one called the gnaw wolf anything but Whistler or the Whistler. He had already been promoted to lieutenant, the second-highest officer at the watch. There was no wolf quite like him.

The Whistler had just done a double shift on the Watch and was terribly tired. And yet he could not sleep. He missed his friends, not only Faolan, but also Edme and Faolan's two sisters. He walked around the spacious cave to pick up the remnants of their scents from when they had all slept here together. When he had sniffed his fill, the pictures on the walls caught his interest, and he wandered down some of the passages he had not yet visited to take a closer look. One spot in particular drew him close. It showed a *byrrgis*, a hunting party, streaking to the east with a frail old wolf in the lead.

There was something about the image, an age and majesty that made the Whistler feel as if he were at the confluence of two worlds and two histories. The stories swept around him, wrapped him tightly, and for the first time he felt himself bound fast, *ycleped*, by clan scent. But this was not the clan scent of the MacDuncans and their packs; this was an ancient scent of ancient clans and creatures from far away and long ago.

The Whistler followed the wall paintings down into another passage he had never seen before. The glittering mica chips in the stone offered the only light, but he could make out the dim scratching on the walls. It was a large drawing and the Whistler had to back up to see it in its entirety. He could just make out what appeared to be wings, a *hoole*, the ancient wolf word for owl. It appeared to be hovering over what at first glance looked like a mountain, but on closer examination, the Whistler realized it was not a mountain at all, but a bear. A huge grizzly bear curled up in sleep, its muzzle buried under its forearm.

Something flashed in the Whistler's brain. Even with its head partially covered, there was something vaguely familiar about the bear. The Whistler closed his eyes for just a moment, straining to remember.

A violent trembling ripped through the cave, buckling the rock floor and tossing the Whistler in the air. The mica chips glittered before his eyes like a constellation sliding down from the sky. *The star ladder descends, but I can't climb. My legs are caught! Skaarsgard, help me! Help me!* But the darkness enveloped him.

CHAPTER TWO

CASTAWAYS

THE BIGHT OF THE OCEAN, ONCE frozen solid, was now a tumult of crashing waves and ice. *The earthquake must have fractured the ice!* Faolan thought as he skidded across a glistening chunk. He dug his claws in to anchor himself and wildly scanned the thrashing water.

"Mhairie! Dearlea!" he howled at the top of his lungs, trying to throw his voice over the roar of the rampaging glacier and the earth's convulsive eruptions.

There was no longer a coastline, at least not one that he recognized. Everything had ruptured, broken into thousands of pieces. Slabs of ice and hunks of earth were piled atop one another. Mountains that once rose high with ice-sheathed peaks had collapsed and crumbled.

"Mhairie! Dearlea!" he shouted again. How would he ever see them? The sea was a jumble of ice floes and carcasses of dead animals that had been swept away into the shove of the glacier.

Then a tiny cry scratched through the cacophony of destruction. "We're sinking! We're sinking, Mhairie!"

Was it possible? Faolan swung his head around. "Dearlea! Dearlea!" he roared.

"Faolan! Over here!" Faolan caught the flash of a tail in the heaving seas.

"Urskadamus!" he cursed. It was the tail of a musk ox, the carcass of an animal he'd found a few days before arriving at Broken Talon Point. Now the carcass was adrift and his dear sisters were riding it as if it were a small boat. But there was an enormous rent in the musk ox's side, and it was sinking fast.

"You've got to swim!" he yelled. "Swim now for me. Swim!"

"The waves are so high," Mhairie cried. "Our necks aren't long enough to get above them. We'll drown."

"Swim!" Faolan roared.

And the sound of his voice so frightened the two young she-wolves that they jumped from the musk ox carcass just before it sank. Their jumps were strong and they landed close to the ice floe. Faolan reached out toward Dearlea, who was closest, and dragged her in with his paw.

"Mhairie, hang on to Dearlea!" Strength surged through him. He clamped his muzzle around the top of Dearlea's head, then lunged with his free paw and grabbed Mhairie's snout. He yanked them both toward his ice raft, but they began to slip, their eyes rolling in horror. "Grip!" he shouted. "Every claw — dewclaws, too! Your teeth if you have to!"

Mhairie and Dearlea dug in, their muscles quivering. Finally, they clawed their way onto the floe.

Whole trees that had been upended floated by. There were also several metal objects that might have been torn from the forges of Rogue smith owls and had yet to sink. The debris was carried by wind or current, or shoved along by the immense blocks of ice. It was as if the world were passing them by, and in an odd sense it all seemed like a welcome distraction as Faolan's sisters found their balance.

"Whatever is that?" Mhairie asked as something sodden swept by.

"Oh my goodness," Faolan gasped. "I believe it is a scroll, or what the owls called a book. The owls wrote their stories on paper."

"Not bone?" Dearlea asked.

"I don't think so."

"Where do you think we'll end up?" Mhairie asked.

"Lupus only knows! Just keep digging your claws in, and hold on tight," Faolan replied.

This was not Faolan's first ice floe, as the laws of the clan wolves decreed that a *malcadh* must be cast out at birth, abandoned in a place where it would surely die. If in the rare occurrence the pup survived and found its way back to its clan, it was accepted back as a gnaw wolf. The place of abandonment was called a *tummfraw*, and the wolf who carried the pup away was called the Obea. Obeas were especially knowledgeable about the forsaken places they could leave malformed pups, places pups would die quickly, without suffering, such as moose trails, where pups were sure to be crushed.

Faolan had been born during the icy brink of time between the end of the hunger moons and the beginning of the Cracking Ice Moon. Therefore, the Obea had taken him to a riverbank, where a chunk of ice was his *tummfraw*. When the watercourse had swollen over the banks, the ice had torn loose and Faolan had ridden an ice cart down a raging cataract of water until he finally, and miraculously, fetched up on the hind paw of the grizzly bear Thunderheart. She was grieving by the river because, two days before, her cub had been snatched by a cougar. Her milk was still flowing and so when Thunderheart adopted the tiny wolf pup, she became his second Milk Giver.

Now Faolan was adrift once again, and his situation no less perilous. He had grown bigger and much stronger, but his grip seemed less firm on the ice. He wondered why. How could he be weaker now than when he was a newborn, his eyes still sealed as he had ricocheted down that river?

"Faolan, look! Look at your paw!"

A most peculiar feeling flooded Faolan's marrow. His paw felt different, but he dared not look at it. *Could it be? Could it mean —?* It was unimaginable.

The wolves had a prophecy that when the ember at the Ring of Sacred Volcanoes was destroyed, all that was bent would be straight, all that was broken would be mended, and those that were born malformed would be suddenly right. Faolan risked a glance down at his paw. It was no longer splayed, misshapen, and ugly. He felt a sudden disorientation. The entire world had just been rearranged and his paw had as well. His cursed paw. His world reeled around him. He was no longer cursed, but was he blessed? He felt strangely unsteady on this new paw. He even felt a pang of . . . of . . . *What? What is it?* he wondered. Then it struck him. *I'm incomplete!* It was as if part of him were missing, as if this split-second change from cursed to not cursed had taken something vital away.

If the ember had been destroyed as the Ring collapsed, the wolves of the Watch must have been relieved of their guard duties. This could be the only reason that his splayed paw had turned. The same would be true for all the gnaw wolves of the Beyond. Twisted limbs would be straightened, missing ears or eyes or tails restored, broken windpipes mended. The time of the Great Mending had come, but only as the whole earth was breaking.

"Hold on!" Dearlea screeched as Faolan skidded toward the edge of the ice floe in shock.

CHAPTER THREE

A STRANGE VOICE

IN THE DIM LIGHT OF THE MYS-
terious cave on the border between the Beyond and the
Outermost, consciousness crept back to the Whistler. The
terrible shaking had stopped. He had fallen somewhere in
the cave but nothing seemed broken. As his eyes adjusted
to the darkness, he saw a large boulder teetering on a ledge
above him and gasped. He leaped to his feet and moved
out of the way. But had he been the one to gasp? It sounded
as if another creature had emitted the noise. He paused to
listen, but the breathing he heard was surely not his own.
His breath was ragged and when he slept at night, the other
wolves teased him that his snoring sounded like a rock
slide. This breathing was soft and even. How very odd.

"Hello! Hello out there!" he called. And now his legs
began to wobble. Something had possessed him, for that
voice was not his, not his at all. His voice was always

hoarse and jagged, but ironically his howling was the loveliest of all the wolves. Somehow the hole in his throat caught the air just right, giving his howl a deep resonance that shivered through the fur of all wolves who heard it.

He decided to try a howl. He opened his mouth and felt the wind pass through his throat in a manner he had never experienced. It felt good and yet it was harder to control the sound. *Well, that's going to take a little work,* the Whistler thought. He rocked back onto his haunches as it hit him. *My hole is . . . is patched! It can't be.* The Whistler opened his eyes in amazement. *The Great Mending . . . has it begun?*

The Whistler was suddenly desperate to get out of the cave, but everything was jumbled, passages blocked. Huge cracks fractured the walls. Oddly enough, none of the pictures, at least that he could see, had been damaged. Not a crack! He remembered the stirring images of the old wolf, the owl, and the bear he had found. That seemed to be part of some sort of very important story. But he couldn't see them and now all he wanted to do was get out. Get out!

He began to tremble. *To die in here, in this dark place? No!* Whistler threw back his head and howled, howled until his newly mended throat felt raw.

"I am at last born whole, but the world has fractured. How can this be? How can it be?" he cried.

CHAPTER FOUR

A Tail Reclaimed

DEEP IN THE OUTERMOST, THAT
most lawless place where wolves ganged together in routs,
an old wolf word that meant "viscious," there was a den
where two routs had camped. The yellow wolf Heep was
strutting about wagging his newly acquired tail. He could
not help but admire it and found it difficult to stop turning his head as if to check it was still there. To his mind,
it was the finishing touch to his leadership here in the
Outermost. In the year or so since he arrived, he had
acquired more power than any other outclanner wolf. In
part, he had to give credit to his time in the Beyond as a
gnaw wolf in the MacDuncan clan. He had been the first
wolf in many years who had actually come to the Outermost
having experienced an extended period of clan life. Most
of the other outclanners had found their way to the region
as either lone wolves or young wolves whose mothers had

died in their whelping dens. These outclanner wolves knew nothing of rank and were without organization of any kind. When Heep arrived, he was smart enough to realize that the outclanner wolves needed at least some kind of order. He set out to try to build what he called a society, but what he actually thought of as a force.

He had built his force one wolf at a time and had so far been fairly successful in bringing two routs together. During the worst of the famine, it had been his idea to set up watches so they could prey on weak clan wolves when they fell into unconsciousness. Wolf eating wolf was not abhorred in the Outermost as it was in the Beyond, and in times of famine, the cannibalism had increased.

So as the other wolves died, Heep and his two routs had thrived, even grown fat. For Heep, it was more than mere survival. In his strange, twisted mind, he relished consuming the flesh of the wolves who had abused him when he was a gnaw wolf in the Beyond. Each bite of their meat brought him an incredible, nearly maniacal surge of power.

Heep was clever. He had even turned two clan wolves who had been following the Prophet. Finding them on the brink of death, perhaps hastened to that brink by out-clanners' teeth and claws, he had nursed them back to health. The wolves were eternally grateful, and naturally, they swore their allegiance.

One of the clan wolves was a she-wolf whom he had rescued and taken as mate even though she was older. Now they had a pup; he was a father. It pleased him greatly although his son had much to learn. He was rather a mealy-mouthed little fellow, with a trace of the *moldwarp* about him. It would be intolerable if the pup didn't grow out of it, but Heep would deal with that later. Heep's sway over his followers was strong, but in his mind it had become even more powerful since the earthquake. That night, just hours before the quake, Heep and his rout had dragged the body of a wolf into the abandoned den of a cougar. The smell of cougar was still redolent in the air.

"Sir," Rags said, assuming a submissive posture — something the outclanners had never done in the past but were learning now. "May I do the honors?" Heep nodded at the large red wolf then turned and winked at his mate, Aliac. She had been helpful in tutoring the rout wolves in decorum. But what Rags did next was a lesson no clan wolf had ever learned. It was a new "tradition" that Heep had introduced and Rags, with his uncommonly long and very sharp fangs, executed skillfully. With one quick bite, Rags snapped off the tail of the dead wolf. Heep had no tail and he made it understood that every wolf killed was to have its tail removed and brought to him. And he did not limit himself to wolf tails. If he joined a *craw*, which was an outclanner blood sport in which they pitted two animals in a fight to the death, Heep made a point of collecting the victim's tail. He had hundreds of them and he kept them in some secret place in the Outermost.

But on that particular evening, just as Rags was about to present the dead wolf's tail to Heep, the earth began to shake violently.

"Out! Out!" Heep shouted. The den's ceiling shuddered above them, and Heep feared they would be smothered. The rout wolves streaked from the den. Two wolves were crushed by tumbling boulders and another disappeared into a gash that had opened in the earth.

"Aliac! Aliac!" Heep cried.

"I'm safe! Safe here with Abban!" she shouted back.

The air was thick with pulverized rock and grime as the earth continued to belch forth its innards. But suddenly Heep had become aware of a strange feeling in his hindquarters, a prickling as if he had backed into a thorn bush. Even as the earth heaved beneath his feet, he whipped around and blinked. The earth shook his brains and the air was thick with dust, but he had seen an unmistakable bump forming on his rump exactly where a tail would have grown. *This cannot be!* he thought. But the bump had grown, lengthened, and soon a white tip poked out. "I am growing a tail!" he gasped. "A tail at last!" He knew what this meant. The earthquake had destroyed the ember and the prophecy of the first king Hoole had come true. That which was broken was being mended. The whole world was broken, but he was mended. He had a tail!

Death and suffering surrounded him, but Heep had never been so happy in his life. He had a tail! In the days after the earthquake, he became mesmerized by it. He practiced constantly flicking it this way and that way. And when no one else was looking, he tried tucking it between his legs in a gesture of submission just for the fun of it. He used his tail to swat his son, which Abban found preferable to being struck by his father's paw. Heep forced his mate, Aliac, to spend countless hours grooming it. He loved that the tip of his tail was white and not the same color as the rest of his pelt. He felt it made a very striking, more commanding, impression.

This, of course, was his mistake. Quietly the other outclanners sniggered behind his back. His vanity was eating away at his marrow, they said. And they were right.

Myrrglosch, a young pup who had been at the Ring for less than half a moon, peeked out from the rubble of the earthquake and blinked. "Oh, Lupus!" he breathed. *How can this be happening? Not now, not after all we've been through!*

A wind like a wall of cold bore down upon the Ring, stinging his face as he peeked out. Behind it, a great white mountain taller than any volcano crumbled through the smoldering remains of the Ring. Was this what was called a glacier? *The H'rathghar glacier!* Myrr thought, cowering against the trembling earth. It was like a beast, a huge gnashing beast of bristling ice. A white grizzly! He had heard a *skreeleen* story about such a beast that appeared to stomp and chew up whatever was in its way. Its leading edge now was so close that it obliterated the sky.

Myrrglosch opened his jaws to scream but the air filled with a great hissing steam as the ice met the last remains of the volcanoes. It snuffed them out, shoveled them into the screaming earth as easily as a bear trampling through a low bush.

Myrr grew dizzy at the thought and he collapsed in a faint.

He was not sure how long he was unconscious, but when he awoke, he was sure he was dead.

Am I a lochin? He licked his paw and he could feel. Or was he teasing himself? He twisted his head around and nipped his own shoulder.

"Youch!" he barked. He'd bitten so hard he'd drawn his own blood.

"Guess I'm alive," he muttered and began to weep enormous tears. He couldn't help it. Too much had happened in his short lifetime. First his parents had abandoned him and he wasn't even a *malcadh*! He was a perfectly formed, healthy pup, so plump and perfect his mother had called him "Cutie Pup"! But then something awful had begun to happen. The strange wolf with a mask and helmet had appeared, calling himself the Prophet, and Myrr's parents had fallen under his spell. They seemed to forget about the clan, then food, then even their own little pup.

Myrr would never forget that day when he left his parents. He would never forget the bland staring look in his mum's green eyes when the Prophet had been exposed as false in front of her. She hadn't even reacted, and when Myrr begged his parents to pay attention, to snap out of the spell, they had walked away from their only pup as if in a daze. That was when Faolan had picked Myrr up gently by the nape of his neck so he and Edme could take Myrr back to the Ring, where he would be cared for properly.

The two Watch wolves brought him directly into the *gadderheal* at the Ring, to the Fengo himself. Finbar had looked at him kindly and called him "a bit of a miracle," using the Old Wolf term for small miracle, *myrr glosch.* Somehow it had stuck — the best part. *Myrr* for miracle. The pup had had a name once upon a time. A name his parents had given him, but now it seemed as dim and distant as his parents. It was as if it, too, had walked away from him on that day.

Everyone had been so nice to him at the Ring, especially Edme when Faolan had gone off with his sisters. But where was everyone now? *Stop crying!* he ordered himself. He had things to figure out. He had lost track of time. Where were the others? What had happened outside?

Cautiously, he crept from his hole. The entire northern and eastern side of the Ring was covered with the glacier. But the other half of the Ring was charred and buried under burnt rubble. It was as if the Ring had been sliced into two, with half of it black and the other half gleaming white. He took another two steps carefully forward.

In the short time Myrr had been in the Ring, it had become familiar territory to him. There had never been a pup at the Ring in all its history, and he was quickly adopted by everyone from the gruffest old Rogue collier owls with their beaks blackened from diving for coals to the *taigas* who instructed the new gnaw wolves. They all loved him, fussed over him as he made his rounds on starry evenings to watch the dazzling eruptions of the volcanoes. He almost had wished he had been born a *malcadh*, so that he could have competed to become a Watch wolf. The wolves' terrible deformities did not bother him in the least; in his eyes, each one was perfect. But now as he crept a bit farther out from his hole, he wondered if there was a single friend left alive. *And please, Lupus*, he prayed silently, *if there is just one, let it be Edme.* He had never met a sweeter wolf.

Myrr tried to walk, but the ground was so uneven that all he could do was stumble through the wreckage of the Ring. There were chunks of ice and overturned boulders, boulders that had once served as meeting places for the daily business of the Ring. And everywhere there were bones, bones that had tumbled and scattered from the cairns where the wolves stood their watches. The *gadderheal*, where the court of the Watch wolves met, was now sealed beneath a pond of burbling lava. But where was the colliers' perch, where owls often waited outside the *gadderheal* to speak with the Fengo? Where was the bone pit where fresh bones were kept until ready for carving? Where was the *taigas'* lodge where the new gnaw wolves came for their lessons? Where were the grooming beds where the off-duty Watch wolves would gather to pick burrs or cinder flakes from one another's pelts and exchange stories?

The landscape had been splintered. Dead wolves and the bodies of singed owls lay everywhere. Was there a living creature? With each step, Myrr feared finding Edme's body, her head crushed like Colleen, the silver wolf with no ears, or Twistling, the brindled wolf with the funny paw. Her back broken like Snowdon, his strange tongue protruding from his mouth.

Myrr wasn't sure what had happened first, the quaking of the earth or the onslaught of the glacier that had come charging down upon the Ring, its edge bright and glaring and sharp as an owl's talons. And now the Ring was crushed. Everything that had been there yesterday was wrecked today — shattered, cracked, and crumbling. The only defining features were the upended remnants of the caves and dens that served as lodges or gathering spots for the wolves and owls. The bones the wolves had carved, the tools the owls used in their forges, stuck out from the ground like the skeletal remains of lives long gone.

The worst places were the ones where lava spills had seeped out from the crushed volcanoes. The victims of the lava were trapped in the thick flows, frozen in the hot black liquid into postures of terror and eternal anguish. The destruction was so complete, so thorough — that was what was most shocking. *How did I escape? Why should I survive?* Myrr thought. He had not been caught by ice or lava or smashed by a boulder or burned by the torrents of flames that ripped from the volcanoes' craters. Just then he heard a small mewling sound. He whipped his head around, but he couldn't find the source. Everything was so confused. There were rocks he had never seen before, and the ones that he recognized were out of place. He was standing by a large slab that he was sure had formed the roof of the *gadderheal*, but it had slid down a slope and was in front of . . . *That must be Edme's den!* His hackles bristled as hope and fear shot through him. *Could she still be alive?*

"Edme! Edme!" Myrr called. "Are you in there?" All

he could hear in response were whimpers. Myrr scrambled to the top of a heap of rock and bones, bones that were carved and had most likely come from the fallen cairns. He knew he must step carefully for he did not want to cause a further collapse that might crush Edme below in the den she had shared with Faolan. He spied an opening and peered in, pressing his eye against the rock. Blinking several times, he let his vision adjust until he could make out the shadowy shape of a wolf below. Edme! His whole body quivered. He couldn't see any blood, no actual wound on her pelt. She appeared to be sleeping, yet she was fretful and every now and then cried out or sighed as if in deep distress. *She must sense that she is the last one left.*

"Edme," he called out. "Edme! It's me, Myrr. I'm here, too. I'm here!"

Edme seemed to hear him. She stirred and rolled over, slowly opening her single eye. It was then that Myrr realized something was very strange. All of the other wolves he had seen, all the Watch wolves who had once been misshapen — their lives had ended and yet their bodies were whole again. He had walked by so many of them, and yet it was only now that Myrr realized that Colleen, who had been earless, seemed to have ears;

Snowdon's split tongue was no longer split; and Leitha, the beautiful black wolf with only three legs, had miraculously grown her fourth. So why would Edme of all wolves still have just one eye?

"Edme?"

"Is that you, Myrr?" Edme's eye flooded with tears. "Are there any others left?"

Myrr gulped. "I don't think so. Are you all right?"

"Yes. Just a bit . . . a bit . . ." Edme could not think what to say.

"A bit of a miracle I think. *Myrr glosch!*" the little pup replied.

CHAPTER FIVE

WATER WING

"I'M JUST NOT USED TO THIS paw." Faolan stared at it with a mixture of alarm and wonderment. He had managed to cling to the edge of the ice floe and avoid sliding into the sea. The paw that had marked him a *malcadh* had been righted, if such a word could be used, but it seemed completely wrong. "It works differently, this paw."

"It works. That's the important thing," Mhairie said, scanning the waves in front of her. "Which way are we going?"

"Toward the western edge of the bight, if the wind keeps blowing from this direction," Faolan answered.

"B-b-but . . . b-but that white thing . . . that . . . that . . ." Dearlea could hardly form the words to describe the mountain of ice that had sliced through the earth.

"The glacier. The H'rathghar glacier," Faolan said. "Gwynneth told me about it."

"Where has it gone? I mean, I thought we were going to be crushed by it. How could it crash through here so fast? I thought glaciers moved slowly."

"I'm not sure, but I think the earthquake tore it loose. Maybe the water made it go faster." Faolan squinted into the distance. It seemed impossible, but there was no sign of Stormfast or Morgan, the two east-facing volcanoes. There was just an immense band of white against the dark horizon. He turned to Dearlea in astonishment. "We were spared, but Stormfast and Morgan were not."

"What are you talking about?" Mhairie said.

Faolan was as confused as his sisters. His eyes scoured the horizon for any sign of the two volcanoes. One moment there had been a ring of fire and then the glacier just swallowed it. He felt panic rising in him. What about Edme? Edme often guarded Stormfast. She knew that volcano's moods better than any other Watch wolf. But now there was absolutely no sign of it, not a thread of smoke, not a bump on the horizon. Only that loom of white like a band of fog in the distance. Could a glacier travel that fast?

There was an ancient story told by the *skreeleens* called the White Grizzly, about an immense ice bear that ate the ground, the meadows, the mountains. But it was just a story and he never paid it much attention because he loved his second Milk Giver, the grizzly bear Thunderheart, and he disliked legends that made bears into monsters. Now it struck him that the White Grizzly had been a glacier and the story that the *skreeleens* told had really happened.

The wind started to pick up, lashing in from out at sea and howling down upon them. The seas were building, waves cresting high over their heads and then crashing down, almost capsizing their small ice raft. The three wolves crouched low and gripped the ice with their claws so they wouldn't be scraped from the floe. Above, the sky was livid and bruised with dark clouds. An immense wave erupted like a monster from the deep trying to batter the moon.

"Hang on!" Faolan shouted and they clung with all their might as the wave crashed. The ice floe plunged into the water then reared up. Miraculously, the three wolves had all managed to cling on, drenched but alive.

"We're being driven off course!" Faolan shouted.

"What course?" Dearlea yelled back at him.

"I'm a Watch wolf. I must get back to the Ring." *And,* he thought, *I need to see if Edme survived.* Life without Edme was almost unimaginable. The very thought made him gasp. Overhead, the moon glowered and the stars bounced in the sky. *Fool!* they all seemed to rail at him. Watch wolves were not supposed to love, to have mates or families. But he could not deny that he felt something very deep for Edme.

Now some maverick current was swirling them in a direction that would take them far from land. If they could get to the south, the water still seemed frozen, but was it solid enough for them to walk across? The glacier had left a violent track with all sorts of debris in its wake. Whole trees from the vast northern forests floated in the waves, and in shallower parts of the sea immense boulders broke through the water.

"What are you thinking, Faolan?" Dearlea asked.

"I'm thinking that we have to steer this ice floe. If we were closer, I'd say we should swim. But the currents are confusing. I'm not sure we'd make it."

"Steer?" Mhairie said. "What do you mean, 'steer'?"

"Is that an owl word?" Dearlea asked.

"I suppose it's sort of an owl notion. When owls fly they just don't point themselves in the direction they want to go. They have to make adjustments for the wind. Gwynneth told me."

But as Faolan began to explain the idea, he wondered. He seemed to know more about flying than Gwynneth had told him. How would he know, for instance, that an owl must angle its tail to make very small adjustments? "Ruddering," they called it. Ice was buoyant and it could not weigh that much. If he could just "rudder" the ice floe the way an owl rudders its tail feathers and its wings to guide its flight . . .

A branch bobbled by. "Grab that!" Faolan barked and Mhairie snapped it up in her jaws.

"Great, Mhairie!" Faolan clamped his foot down on the branch as soon as she set it on the ice floe. He studied it for several minutes.

"Whatever are you going to do with that?" Dearlea asked.

"First I have to gnaw it."

"But it's not bone, Faolan," Mhairie said, exchanging a worried glance with her sister.

"No. It's not. It's softer than bone. So I have to take my time with it. I don't want to break it." He peered at the branch again. In his mind's eye, a shape grew, something flat but with a slightly curved edge. *How to go about this?* Faolan wondered. He closed his eyes tight. Gnawing a branch would be so different than gnawing a bone.

The wood had soaked up the seawater and was softer than he had anticipated. It gave way under his teeth and become slightly pulpy. But he was not discouraged. He immediately perceived that if he could somehow flatten one end of it into a fan shape, the branch just might do the trick.

"What does this look like to you, Mhairie?" he asked.

"Uh . . . a chewed piece of wood."

"Does it remind you of anything?"

"Beyond a chewed piece of wood?" Mhairie asked.

"Yes. Anything at all come to mind?"

"Not much. Sorry, Faolan." Once more, Mhairie met her sister's eyes.

"If I stuck this on my behind, what would I look like?" he persisted.

"Well, it's shredded. So maybe like a wolf with a chewed piece of wood on his butt?" she guessed.

"True. True, but anything else?" His sisters flicked their ears in dismay. They wanted to help him, but could not figure out what he wanted them to see in this branch with the pulverized end. They shook their heads.

"Sorry, Faolan." Mhairie paused. "But maybe if you could tell us what it reminds you of, we could see it."

"All right. Don't laugh, but it sort of reminds me of tail feathers."

"Ooooh!" cried Dearlea. "I see what you mean now!"

"Why would you want to chew a stick to look like an owl's tail feathers?" Mhairie asked.

"I want to make something so we can control which way this ice floe is taking us. The way owls guide their flight with their wings." Faolan's sisters blinked at him. Then they were silent for a long time, but at least they had not instantly declared him *cag mag*.

"Well," Dearlea said slowly, "you realize that basically owls have three wings, if you think of their tail as one."

"Yes. That's a problem," Faolan conceded.

Dearlea cocked her head. "That branch would be just one wing. You have to chew it up much further so you have something big that can really sweep through the water."

Perhaps it was the word "sweep," but something kindled an image in Faolan's brain. One large, gigantic wing to guide this floe.

"Why, of course! You're a genius, Dearlea!" Faolan looked at the limb. "If I start gnawing about here" — he indicated a point that was a third of the way up the branch — "that would give this wing, this water wing, the pull we need."

"We?" Dearlea and Mhairie both said at once.

"But, Faolan, we're not gnaw wolves," Mhairie protested.

Faolan was stunned. "Do you think it's beneath you?"

Dearlea's tail dropped between her legs. "No, no never!" said Dearlea in a soft voice. "But we know nothing about carving the way you do. And this is very different."

"It's different for me, too," Faolan said, and he looked down at the strange new paw with which he gripped the branch. "Everything is different. Come on, now. Help me out."

His sisters looked at each other and began to gnaw on the piece of wood. It did not take them long to shred the bottom third of the branch.

"Now for the test," Faolan said. The ice floe on which they were floating was not any really regular shape. It somewhat resembled a bulging triangle, with the point of the triangle facing toward the far side of the bight, the direction they wanted to go. Faolan noticed a slight notch on the backside of the floe and thought it might be just about the right size to hold the water wing.

"Help me here," he said to his sisters. "I don't want the currents to pull this away. We all have to hang on to it."

"How will you fit it in?" Dearlea asked.

"Carefully! Get a firm grip on it with your jaws while I try to guide it into this slot."

Water splashed up on the wolves. "Urskadamus!" Faolan muttered as a wave caught him right in the face. He was attempting to grip the ice with one paw and guide the water wing with his other. If only he had his splayed paw back, that blessed paw that had cursed him as a *malcadh*! He knew how to use it, how to turn it. This new paw was good for nothing.

Four, five times he tried to slide the branch into the ice notch and each time he failed. Mhairie and Dearlea never gave up. Even as they gripped the branch in their jaws they spoke encouraging words to him.

"You'll do it, Faolan!" Mhairie mumbled, trying to cheer past the wet wood that filled her mouth.

"Yesh!" Dearlea agreed.

On the fifteenth try, Faolan gave up. "This is impossible. Mhairie, put down the branch and step on it as hard as you can so it's braced and won't slide off."

Dearlea's pelt was shingled with ice. She looked exhausted, but there was a bright, determined light in her eyes. "Faolan, you can do this!"

"Not with this paw. This good-for-nothing paw! I'm just not used to it."

"Faolan," Mhairie snapped. "I have never in all my life heard you whine. Don't start now. You can do it!"

"Quit thinking about your paw and start thinking about the one you had," Dearlea urged. "Let your old paw, the splayed one, teach the new paw." Faolan blinked at his sister.

"That seems odd, doesn't it? Kind of upside down?" Faolan replied.

Dearlea snarled. "Look around you. The whole world has been turned upside down."

"All right. I'll give it another try." Faolan closed his eyes and tried his best to imagine his other paw, to feel how he would have used it to move the branch into that slot in the ice. He saw his old splayed toes, the way the paw turned. He felt it in his mind's eye and then he felt a kind of muscle memory moving his new paw.

"Hold tight!" he cried as the branch slipped into place and caught.

Angle it! Angle it! he thought as he recalled the countless times he had tipped his head skyward and watched Gwynneth carve a turn or negotiate a wind draft. The branch trembled, then suddenly caught the pressure of the current. He bit firmly into the upper part of the limb with his mouth and gave Dearlea and Mhairie a flick of his ears to signal them to let go. He pushed the stick slightly to one side and felt the ice floe move in the opposite direction. *That makes sense*, he thought, getting a hang of it. Then he pushed it the other way and the ice floe clearly responded.

"You're doing it, Faolan!" Mhairie cheered. "You're doing it!"

Yes, he thought, *I am doing it!* But his marrow grew colder and colder as the opposite shore drew closer and he could see the land in utter ruin. The Ring of Sacred Volcanoes, which used to stand so proudly in the distance, had disappeared, collapsed.

But Edme? Where is Edme? Her name wound through his mind like an urgent beat. *Where is she? Where is she?*

The waters calmed as they approached shore and the sun began to rise. But without Edme, what did it mean — a new day.

CHAPTER SIX

ANOTHER PELT

THE SARK HAD BUT ONE THOUGHT in her mind — to get back to her cave in the Slough. That was all she cared about. Her flank was ripped, a bad wound, and it would turn rancid, give her blood poisoning, and undoubtedly kill her, but she had to get back to the Slough and her encampment before then. She wanted to die on her own terms, in her cave within sight of her kiln and all the memory jugs she had made over the course of her very long life. If she could not die with those pots, with the scents they contained that she had collected over a lifetime . . . she dared not finish the thought.

She still wasn't sure what had happened. One minute she had been standing beneath a blue spruce tree in the Shadow Forest with Gwynneth, and the next there was a rumble, and she felt herself heaved a great distance by the convulsions of the earth. The gash in her flank was bleeding heavily, but she had packed it with snow and some precious rabbit-ear moss. This had stopped the flow of blood and she had no broken bones. So the Sark, an ever-practical sort, kept repeating practical words and phrases that ordered her body to continue, to endure. *My legs still work, my sniffer is keen. Praise Lupus, I am still a wolf. Nobody lives forever, but I can and I will make it to the Slough!* Over and over, she repeated these words and urged her broken body on.

The Sark knew that some wolves would say the earthquake was Lupus's revenge on the faithless. But the Sark did not believe such nonsense. She wasn't even sure she believed in a Cave of Souls, Skaarsgard, or the Great Star Wolf Lupus himself. She was too practical to ever subscribe to the elaborate codes of tradition and laws that guided every aspect of clan wolf life. The only thing truly sacred to the Sark was memory, which she considered the very marrow of a decent life. And the key to her memories was scent.

The Sark's sense of smell was legendary in the Beyond, and she was using it now to guide her through the ruined landscape and back toward her home.

The scents had been disturbed because of the sulfurous odors wafting across the Beyond from the eruptions at the Ring. It seemed, the Sark reflected, as if the earth had a bad tummy ache. What was the wonderful expression the owls had for that? She tried to remember for a moment *Ah, yes — the "yarpie barpies."* Sometimes the owls really did strike the right note with language. "Tummy ache" was such a weak, pusillanimous phrase. But it was as if the earth needed a gigantic dose of her special mixture of henbane and mint, which she often gave to wolves with the scours.

Time stopped having much meaning for the Sark. Although the sun tracked against the sky, there was a veil of ash in the air that made it seem as if she were moving through a perpetual twilight. She didn't feel hunger or pain, but she made herself eat the leg of a dead marmot she had come upon. She knew she had to keep up her strength if she wanted to make it back to the Slough alive.

What she needed even more than food was rabbit-ear moss. The wound in her flank had opened up again and she could not sustain too much blood loss. But she soon came upon a stand of birch trees that had been upended and it gave her an idea. Well-chewed birch bark was something she kept a good supply of in her cave for the wolves who sought her out after sustaining an injury from an elk or moose in a *byrrgis*.

47

And so the Sark paused to chew the birch bark into a pulpy mass, which she then stuffed into the angry hole in her side. As she chewed, she wondered about Faolan. She'd taken a liking to him ever since she had first encountered him as a young pup. Because of the odd tracks left by his splayed paw, the clans had thought he had the foaming-mouth disease and had tried to track him down and kill him. *What a wolf! By my stars*, she thought, *I hope he's survived. A wolf like him only comes along once in a thousand years.* The thought set the Sark's cag mag eye to spinning. *Once in a thousand years*, the words rang in her head like distant chimes. A long time ago, the Sark had whispered into a memory jug a strange question. *Could Faolan be a* gyre *soul?*

She remembered the exact pot she had pressed her muzzle against. It had a green glaze made from the silt near the south bend of the big river and its shape was so fetching and slender. A keening coursed through her. *I must get back to my pots!*

Faolan and his sisters had made shore in the early morning and spent the day picking their way across the fractured landscape on shaking legs. The thought of

Edme and the Ring drove Faolan on, but as night set, his sisters protested. The three wolves were exhausted and needed rest. Still, sleep could not come easily on broken ground that still quivered now and then with aftershocks.

The Great Bear constellation seemed to sway overhead, drawing Faolan back to those summer nights he spent under the stars with Thunderheart. Thunderheart had first pointed out the Great Bear constellation to Faolan when he was just a pup. Odd he had not thought about that in years. *What was it she said?* Suspended halfway between sleep and dream, he struggled to recall the conversation. She had been telling him something about how to follow the last claw on the Great Bear's paw to find the star that never moves. *The Outermost is in between that claw and the star the owls call NeverMoves. I once had a den there. Someday . . .*

Someday what? Faolan had asked. Thunderheart looked troubled and didn't answer.

Someday we'll go back? he'd persisted.

Perhaps. But I am not sure if it is good for your kind.

My kind?

My kind, my kind . . . The words rumbled through his head, his bloodstream, his marrow, and then through a heart as huge and sonorous as that of his grizzly bear Milk Giver.

His pelt was no longer silver, but a thick rough brown — the pelt of a bear. He saw himself clearly now, not as a little wolf pup but as a huge grizzly swimming in a golden river in the time of the Salmon Moon.

He heard the alarm roar of a female grizzly. Her cubs were being threatened. He dropped the fish clamped in his jaws and clambered onto the banks to see the standoff between the mother grizzly and a moose. He roared, his whole body trembling with the great noise. But the moose stood there unmoving, then suddenly lowered his head. The full rack of immense antlers rushed toward him. If he reared, he would give the moose a larger target, so he crouched, rolled, and shot out his immense forepaw just as the animal passed by. The moose's front leg popped from the shoulder socket, and the moose let out a terrible bellow. His leg flopped on the ground as if it belonged to another animal entirely.

Eo, for that was Faolan's bear name, came up to the moose and tore the limb from its shoulder with one swift stroke. He lashed out with his paw and slashed open the moose's chest, tearing out its heart. The animal felt no more pain.

There is something else I must do, Eo thought. He had a vague recollection of some other rite, a ceremony, but it was too late for lochinvyrr, *the gratitude of the predator toward its prey. And why did he even think of* lochinvyrr? Lochinvyrr *was a wolf ritual, not one for bears.* "I am a bear," *he said.* "A bear."

The wisps of Eo's memories rose up in Faolan, enveloping him like wraiths from another lifetime. They were real and not imagined, he had lived the life of a bear.

I was a bear! I chose to be a bear! That was part of my secret, I chose to be a bear. He was not Thunderheart. He was not Faolan. *It was Eo who killed the moose. I am Eo! I was Eo!*

"Faolan, wake up! It's time to get moving again. Wake up." Mhairie nudged him gently.

He blinked, then looked at his sisters and wondered if they knew what he had dreamed. What he had been. Did they see the wolf, or the bear that lived within him?

CHAPTER SEVEN

OUT OF CHAOS

ALL GWYNNETH'S OLD LANDMARKS were gone, erased. The night of the earthquake, she had used the stars to navigate. But the stars were soon enough swallowed by the daylight, and it was a daylight like none Gwynneth had ever seen, for the air was filled with ash and bits of dust. It was as if the most enormous grizzly bear imaginable had been seized with the foaming-mouth disease and had run amok across the world.

She flew low over the land, swooping into the huge gashes that plunged to enormous depths. "Sark! Sark!" she called. "Where are you?" But she heard nothing and she was so disoriented she knew she might be flying in circles.

Her first task was to orient herself in this new landscape, for she would have no guides or signposts until the stars came out again. Unlike a wolf, she had no sense of smell that might give her clues. She knew that the sun rose in the east and set in the west, but the scrim of ash was so thick it was hard to determine where the light was coming from.

She settled for flying in ever-widening circles around the uprooted spruce tree. It helped her get her bearings slightly and she felt fairly sure she knew the direction of the Ring of Sacred Volcanoes. But as she tipped her head toward what she thought was north, she couldn't see the crowns of the volcanoes. When the quake had happened, the sky had ignited with volcanic flames and flashes. There were sparks and plumes of smoke still in the air in that direction, but she couldn't make out one of the distinctive profiles of the volcanoes.

Aftershocks and tremors were still trembling across the land, and she could hear the rumbles and belchings of the earth. But her ear slits caught another sound, a tiny one that seeped through the earth's growlings. Gwynneth tipped her head and angled her ear slits to catch these faint noises. It was as if she were sifting through the din of the catastrophe to capture a sliver of feeble mewlings. *This cannot be!* she thought. *That could not happen at a time like this!* But Glaux, if it didn't sound like a newborn wolf pup!

The masked owl realized that she had unwittingly come close to her own forge. Indeed the sound was coming from her forge. It was hard to recognize at first because the place had been flattened. The den she had excavated for her living space and tools was partially blocked by fallen trees that had been uprooted just like the blue spruce in the Shadow Forest. But still, the mewling was coming from inside.

Gwynneth had been away from her home for some time before the earthquake. There had been so few caribou herds passing through to provide caribou scat for her forge that she had temporarily taken up residence in her auntie's old place in Silverveil. She supposed she should not begrudge another creature availing itself of the comforts of her home, but she sensed the creature had been there for some time.

Gwynneth fluffed her feathers. She was uncertain how she should announce her presence. Several of her tools were scattered about — her coal bucket, her tongs, and one of her two favorite hammers. She wondered where the other was.

There was a sudden intake of breath from the inside. The mewling continued, but whoever gasped was aware of Gwynneth's presence and didn't dare come out of the den. Gwynneth cocked her head to one side, then the other. She picked up two heartbeats, one from a very tiny heart, the other beat stronger and accelerated. Tree branches had been purposefully dragged across the burrow to camouflage the entrance.

"Hrrh hrrr," Gwynneth made a polite clearing sound in her throat. "Pardon me for intruding — although this happens to be my home. Would you like to come out or should I come in?"

"I can't come out right now. I hope you'll understand, Gwynneth."

The Masked Owl swiveled her head almost entirely around and then flipped it upside down and backward, as only owls can do because of the extra bones in their necks. She recognized the voice, but the tone was entirely different!

"Banja!"

"I know, I know!" Banja looked up as the Masked Owl entered the den and stood dumbfounded before a scene that struck her as not simply odd, but almost miraculous. To think that in a land plagued for over a year by famine and then cursed with an earthquake, this could have happened! The nastiest she-wolf at the Watch had at her teat the most darling little she-pup. Banja, of all wolves, was a mother! Gwynneth blinked in dismay. Watch wolves were not allowed to find mates for fear their affliction would be carried on in their offspring.

Like Edme, Banja had but one eye. There the resemblance ended; the red wolf was as nasty as Edme was kind. Spiteful, jealous, always eager to cast blame or fight — and now here she was, cuddling a newborn pup whose pelt was as gold as autumn grass.

"Whhh-wwhhh-what's all this?" Gwynneth's beak trembled.

"This is Maud — Maudie, I call her. And I am her mum." The way Banja said these words was enough to make Gwynneth's gizzard melt.

"May I come closer?" Gwynneth asked.

"Yes, of course. Come take a peek."

Gwynneth hopped closer and peered down at the little creature. "She's lovely, Banja. Just lovely."

"And look, Gwynneth. She has two eyes! They're still sealed now. But I peeked beneath both lids and they're both there! She's not like me at all!" Banja's head drooped. "The Fengo will forgive me. I know I have broken the most serious of all the codes that govern the Ring. But even if he discharges me, that's okay. I really just want to be a mum."

"I wouldn't worry."

"What do you mean?"

"How long have you been here?"

"A while now. I came before the earthquake. I know this sounds . . . terrible . . . but I had to eat. I had to eat so Maudie could be born. I did some hoarding, but for a good cause. For Maudie. I know it's bad! But I'm going to tell the Fengo everything."

"I don't think the Fengo will say anything," Gwynneth said gently. "I can't see the Ring. I think it's gone."

Banja blinked. Her mouth dropped open. She tilted her head to one side, as if she were trying to comprehend the words that had just been spoken.

"Gone?" Her mouth wobbled as if it were having trouble shaping the word. "Gone?"

"And there's more."

"Wh-wh-what?" Banja was too shocked to reply coherently.

"Maudie is like you."

Banja's hackles bristled. "How dare you?" Her voice scraped the air.

"You, my dear Banja, have two eyes now, just like Maudie."

"What?" Banja blinked rapidly.

"The prophecy, Banja! The ember has been released and the Ring has been destroyed. It is the time of the mending, the Great Mending."

Banja was stunned. She blinked her good eye and then slowly, as if it couldn't possibly be true, blinked the eye that had always been missing. She immediately snapped both eyes shut and sat frozen for more than a minute.

"Where do we go from here?" Banja asked when she was ready.

"That's a good question. It's a different world out there now, Banja. A new world."

"And I am a new wolf." She nuzzled her golden pup.

Out of all this chaos, some good has come, Gwynneth thought, and sent a prayer out to her missing friends.

CHAPTER EIGHT

THE BROKEN RING

IT HAD BEEN BARELY HALF A MOON since Faolan had been at the Ring of Sacred Volcanoes, but everything had changed. It was not simply that the volcanoes had collapsed. There were textures at the Ring that Faolan would always remember — the way the black sand of crushed lava felt between his paws, the gritty sound it made when blown by the wind, the plumy softness of the deep ash beds. But none of that remained. Faolan walked through the still-smoldering ruins of what had been the Ring of Sacred Volcanoes, his sisters by his side.

"Be careful! That lava is running hot," Faolan cautioned Dearlea as she veered close to the wreckage of Stormfast. Or was it Morgan? Faolan found it impossible to fix his bearings.

They passed the scorched remains of two Rogue

smiths, their blackened talons still clutching their tools. One held fast to his tongs, the other a hammer. Faolan stopped to study them, dread flooding his stomach. But neither one was Gwynneth. Faolan shut his eyes. *Let her be safe. Let them all be safe*, he prayed.

He looked down again at the two smiths. In all the tumult, how had they managed to cling to their tools? The collier's art was diving into forest fires to retrieve prize embers and coals. They knew how to negotiate tricky cross drafts, plunge between the tongues of flames for the freshest coals without singeing a feather. He hoped most of the owls, at least, had survived.

But there was not an owl aloft in the sky and not a Watch wolf to be seen. The cairns on which the wolves had stood their watches were annihilated. An eerie silence enveloped everything. Gone were the deep rumbles of the quake and the pervasive gurglings of the boiling lava cauldrons; the sizzles of coals and embers were mere whispers now as they cooled with no colliers to retrieve them.

"Malachy!" Faolan gasped as he spotted the body of the *taiga* with the crooked hips, who was the Ring's expert on the owls and their ways. Malachy was pressed beneath a boulder, his head bashed in. But how odd that in death his hips now seemed straighter than they ever had in life. Near him was the body of Conny, a short-eared owl from the Great Tree, who was a distinguished collier. It was said that he had learned from King Soren, the best collier the tree had ever seen.

If they are gone . . . if a strong flyer like Conny couldn't escape . . . how could Edme survive? With each step, a dark dread rose within him.

"Edme!" His bark scratched the air. "Edme!" He barked again. There was a rustling sound from a pile of rock fragments, then a small explosion of dust and ash hurled toward him.

"Faolan! You're safe." And like a little whirlwind behind her came Myrr, yipping happily. "You're here!" Edme exclaimed. Her whole body quivered with joy.

"You're alive!" Faolan said. His eyes were brilliant with his panic and relief. "You're alive!" He began to sniff her all over, as if to convince himself the wolf before him was really his dear friend. His fellow Watch mate, but something else trembled in his marrow. *She is more than that, much more than a Watch mate!*

"Edme, Edme!" He couldn't stop repeating her name.

"Faolan, your paw!" she gasped. "The time of the mending — it has come." A tear sprang to her eye. She shrugged and gave a halfhearted chuckle. "But not for me. Remember, I am a *malcadh* made, not born." Her face flinched and she looked away almost as if she were trying to hide her single eye. As if she felt embarrassed, as if the failure were hers. Faolan couldn't bear it. He took a step closer and licked her tear away. She shivered at the touch of his tongue on her face.

"Your eye was ripped from you when you were so young. It's not your fault. And you see more with your single eye than any wolf with two. You are the wolf dearest to me."

"What's this we're eating?" Faolan said when they had settled into the makeshift den that Edme had organized.

"Lemming," Edme replied. "It's odd to think that before the earthquake we were all starving. But the glacier dug up all these little rodents."

"I don't understand," Faolan said. "Half of the Ring looks like ice now."

"I think the glacier broke through here, ruptured or something. There was another tremor here last evening and Myrr and I saw a crack. The front of the glacier slipped off, just slid away from this chunk. We watched until it was almost out of sight."

Myrr came up wagging his tail. "It's like the White Grizzly," he said.

"Oh, that story," Faolan replied quietly. *And what happens when old legends come to pass, when they come true?*

"As far as I can tell, it passed north of here," Edme continued. "It crashed straight through the MacDuncan territory, shoved west right over Crooked Back Ridge. The glacier leaves a huge track and along its edges there were these little rodents. I finished off the dying ones and Myrr and I brought them back." She paused. "It's so awful. After all those moons of famine we find all this food and there's only us to eat it."

"You can't mean that everyone is dead?" He began to splutter, "I saw Malachy and Conny, but . . . but . . . All the Watch wolves?"

"The Fengo is dead," Edme said.

Mhairie and Dearlea gasped. "The Fengo, dead?"

Edme nodded. "I set out his body where the drying place for bones used to be. There are still vultures about and they have made short work of it. His bones are almost bare."

"He should be on the cairn of the Fengos," Faolan mourned.

"But that's the queerest thing of all. The cairn still stands!"

Faolan met her solemn gaze. "Then we need to place Finbar's bones there when they are ready. We need to do his final ceremony. Do you remember how it is done from the Bone of Bones?"

Edme looked at Faolan. Her single eye shone brightly. "The Ring might be broken, but its spirit is not."

CHAPTER NINE

THE CAIRN
OF THE FENGOS

THE FIVE WOLVES STOOD IN A
circle just as the curve of the moon slid up on the horizon
like a thin, sparkling blade. The fog of their breathing
misted the air of the circle as they huddled together. Their
postures were those of grieving wolves, their tails droop-
ing as if they lacked the strength to hold them properly.
Their muzzles trembled. Their hackles were raised and their
ears shoved forward just a bit as if perhaps they were waiting for the whispery drift that was said to pass when a
lochin came one's way. Edme's bright green eye glistened
with tears as she began to recite the Fengos' ritual from
the Bone of Bones.

"Since the time of the first Fengo, it has been commanded that the weathered bones of the Ring's chieftain
be brought to the cairn, along with any bones he has

carved during his lifetime." Edme looked over at Faolan. "Do you think his bones are ready, Faolan?" He nodded, and she continued, "We stand watch the first night in case the bones attract a scavenger."

Edme closed her eyes for several seconds. She was recalling a night from three moons before when she and Faolan had been out scouting, taking turns hunting for tracks. While she waited for him in the den they had found during one of the worst blizzards, she had become aware of a presence. She looked up expecting Faolan, but instead she saw something that rattled her to the marrow. It was a huge but ancient wolf who seemed to glow like a *lochin*.

But the real shock was that the wolf before her was not a *lochin* come down from the Cave of Souls. It was Faolan come in from the blizzard, his pelt stiff with frost. Nevertheless, she had sensed a secret, a visit from a presence older than time.

"Faolan, you should be the one to stand the watch."

Faolan said nothing, but nodded. He knew she was right.

So, in the trickling light of the sickle moon, the four wolves and the pup, Myrr, transported the bones of the last Fengo of the Ring from the drying beds to the cairn of the Fengos.

"Give Myrrglosch that bone," Faolan said. "Let the bit of a miracle place the Fengo's last bone." He nodded at the cairn of the Fengos, which still stood erect and whole despite the earthquake.

As soon as Myrr placed the last bone, the five wolves sank down to the ground and covered their eyes with their paws, a gesture of utmost submission to the highest authority. Then, rising, but with their tails still tucked and their eyes still shut, they tipped back their heads and howled at the dim splinter of the moon. As Watch wolves of the Ring, Faolan and Edme were the only ones who knew the howls that had been incised on the Bone of Bones. But little Myrr listened carefully. He would not howl, but he whispered the phrases to himself.

"Lupus, guardian of the Cave of Souls, Skaarsgard, keeper of the star ladder, here lie the bones of your humble servant Finbar Fengo, watcher of the Watch that was begun in the time of the first Fengo, who led our clans out of the Long Cold on the Ice March. Guide Finbar's spirit now to the star ladder to follow in the tracks of Hamish, Fengo before Finbar, and then that of O'Meg and that of Pegoth." Faolan and Edme continued reciting until they had named all the Fengos for a thousand years. By the time they had finished, the sliver of the moonlight had slid away to another world and all was dark.

Edme, Mhairie, Dearlea, and Myrr went to a new den nearby that Edme had dug out from the rubble, and Faolan settled down to guard the cairn of the Fengos. He was not tired at all, but his mind was divided. While one part kept watch, the other slipped into a kind of waking dream that had started when he and Edme had begun to recite the names of the Fengos.

In his dream, Faolan saw a Spotted Owl perched near the wolf. The owl was battle weary, yet listened with rapt attention to what the old wolf was saying. There was a closeness, a compelling confidence between the two creatures. Their heads were bent toward each other so they nearly touched. Faolan could almost catch threads of their conversation.

"You came to learn about fire, did you not? I can help you," *the old wolf was saying.* "I can teach you some things, but not everything, Grank."

Grank! *The name reverberated in Faolan's head and his marrow quickened.*

The owl named Grank seemed puzzled at the old wolf's

words. "How can that be, Fengo? How can you help me learn more . . . about fire?"

In his dream, Faolan was dimly aware that Fengo was the wolf's name, not his title. What was he witnessing in his dream? Had he gone back to the very origins of the Ring, more than a thousand years ago?

The owl addressed the wolf as an equal with no honorifics. Faolan was so far back in history that there was no Watch at the Ring. The only wolf was a plain old gray named Fengo.

"You are able to fly over craters from which the fire leaps. You can look into the heart of a volcano. On the wing, you could catch the hottest coals."

Soon the voices dwindled and the mournful strand of a wolf's glaffling wove through the night. The old wolf was sitting alone on a ridge, his head thrown back howling the strange mad music of grief. There was no trace of the Spotted Owl.

Where is he? Where is he? Where is Grank?

Never gone so long.

Has he been killed?

Does he now climb the spirit trail, Lupus?

When the song ended, the mists rose and the wolf on the ridge had changed again and appeared older. An owl that was not Grank flew off with an ember in its beak — a green ember with a lick of blue at its center. The Ember of Hoole! The first king had been anointed. The old wolf could rest now.

But though Fengo's spirit longed to slip from his pelt, it was not quite over. Faolan felt the marrow leaking from him, a cool wind whistling through his bones. They were becoming hollow. Deep in his belly he felt a small spark, a kindling. I have a gizzard! I am becoming an owl! I chose to be an owl — a Snowy Owl!

The beak opened and a beautiful sound ribboned the air. Song! It was at that moment the owl realized something else was very different. I am female! I chose this, too. I am back . . . I am back, she thought. The wind ruffled through her feathers. She felt so light, so free. She angled her wings steeply and swept into a deep banking turn. The sky tilted and the moon winked from behind a cloud. The constellation of the Little Raccoon was rising and she could almost brush its forepaws with her wing tips. The wind shivered through her delicate face feathers. She blinked her eyes and a thin membrane wiped across them clearing her vision. As she flew, it felt as if she were embracing the whole world, the entire universe.

She looked down. She was flying over the Sea of Hoolemere. Over the spreading crown of the Great Ga'Hoole Tree. Fengo had long been dead. The first king long dead. A new king ruled.

She alighted in the Great Tree and quickly found her way
to Madam Plonk, the Great Tree's renowned singer. Madam
Plonk was poring over her "collectibles," as she called her vast
assortment of silly doodads she got from Trader Mags.

"Brunwella?"

The Snowy Owl wheeled about as she heard her name.

"Fee!"

"Yes."

"What a surprise, but do call me Madam Plonk, dear.
It's a bit more formal around here. Now, I hope you're
coming with good news?"

"If you mean am I going to stay, no," *the owl replied.*

"But, Fionula, I am going to need your help. This is a
big job. They have let the job of tree singer go vacant for
too long. The grass harp needs to be tuned. The blind
snakes instructed."

"I can stay for a little bit, but you know as well as I
that in my gizzard I am and always shall be a gadfeather."

Madam Plonk sighed. "You gadfeathers can't keep still.
Restless creatures, the lot of you."

What Madam Plonk had said about restlessness had
more than a grain of truth in it. It was, however, not simply
a matter of place. There was something deeply restless in
Fionula's gizzard. I have a restless soul. *Something flashed*

in her mind's eye. The figure of a wolf with a tattered pelt. "Brunwella, I mean Madam Plonk, have you met the new Fengo of the Watch yet?"

"No. You know I don't get on with wolves that well." *Fionula winced.* "It's not that I don't like them exactly, I just . . . I can't explain it. All that business they do with bones. Why don't they just swallow them like we do? Get them wrapped up in a nice little pellet and yarp the whole business? But, no, they make such a . . . a . . ." *Madam Plonk was searching for the right word.* "A fetish really, carving them and all that. Seems silly."

"Not to them!" *Fionula replied sharply.*

"Now, don't get huffy. You'd think you were a wolf or something. I just have to say that I don't care a bit for their odor." *Madam Plonk had now plucked up a strand of black pearls and was draping them over her shoulders.*

"What about their odor, what's wrong with it?" *Fionula said.*

"Meat. Too much meat in their diet."

"We eat meat."

"Yes, but not big meat like they do. And we cook a lot of ours."

"Well, we have fire, or here at the tree you do at least. And the wolves don't."

"They have plenty of fire over at the Ring of Sacred Volcanoes. More fire than they know what to do with."

Fionula felt her gizzard stir. Her feathers puffed up. "It would be against the *gaddernock* for them to cook their meat using embers from the Ring of Sacred Volcanoes. They guard those volcanoes. The Bone of Bones, third *gwalyd* — 'No embers from the coals of any of the five volcanoes shall be used by wolves for the purpose of cooking meat. Only owls may use these coals for their iron mongering. If owls wish to cook meat, they must bring to the Ring coals from forest fires.'"

"Now, how ever do you know that, Fionula? Bone of Bones, what's that all about?"

Fionula shook her head and blinked several times. Her yellow eyes grew dim. "I don't know how. I just do."

The sun was just bleaching the eastern sky when Edme came out of the den.

"Did you sleep at all, Faolan?"

"Not really, but I'm fine," he answered.

Edme cocked her head at him. "Are you sure?"

"Yes, but . . ." Faolan hesitated. "Edme, there's nothing left here. We have to move on. Go."

"Go?" Her pelt bristled in astonishment. "Go where?"

"West. We have to find the Sark, if we can. And the Whistler at the Blood Watch."

Edme met his eyes steadily, and Faolan knew she understood. "But that's not all you have in mind, is it?"

He shook his head. "We're going much farther west."

"Farther west?" Dearlea had just come out from the den, her sister right behind her.

"You mean to the Outermost? Surely not!" Mhairie gasped. But she saw a faraway look in her brother's eyes.

"I mean beyond the Outermost," Faolan replied. "I mean . . . I mean . . ." his voice began to ebb.

"Faolan?" Edme whispered. "What are you seeing?"

When he answered, his voice was strong again. "Once, on a very clear day when I stood on the Blood Watch, I turned west and I saw beyond the Outermost, almost all the way across the western sea." He paused. "I saw the Distant Blue."

"The Distant Blue?" Dearlea echoed.

"I don't know its true name, but I call it that. The Distant Blue is where we must go."

The wolves fell silent as they looked at him. The Beyond was broken, the earth fractured beneath their feet. But where was Faolan taking them?

CHAPTER TEN

ALMOST AS GOOD
AS TWO EYES

WHERE DO WE GO FROM HERE? BANJA'S question thrummed in Gwynneth's head as she flew. She had promised Banja that she would return, but Gwynneth needed to search for the Sark, and for Faolan and Edme. Was there any chance they could still be alive?

She was shocked when she looked down on what used to be Crooked Back Ridge. It was not simply flattened by the glacier, but the earth had been gouged out to an enormous depth. Parts of it were no longer a ridge, but a deep valley. The glacier, only half a league past the ridge and slowing now, had left an immense cleft in its wake.

A galloping glacier! Gwynneth thought. She had heard about them when she was in the northern kingdoms but never actually seen one. And then there was the old *skreeleen* tale of the White Grizzly.

Everywhere there were deep cuts, deadly crevasses. Being an owl, Gwynneth could swoop down into many of these and she saw that they had become death traps for elk, moose, marmots, and many wolves. The crevices were a carrion feeder's delight, but the sight of these birds revolted Gwynneth. She remembered her father speaking of the vultures who had scoured the battlefield after the last of the Great Owl wars, the War of the Ember. She could not abide the idea. She plunged now into a crevice and with an ear-shattering shree flew directly at two vultures who were feeding on the body of a wolf.

She attacked with outstretched talons and managed to rake the eye of the smaller vulture. That was enough to scare them both off. But it was only after the vultures had flown away that Gwynneth recognized the wolf whose carcass they had all but destroyed. "Oona," she whispered. "Great Glaux, it is Oona!" The black wolf had been a fearless lieutenant from the MacNamara clan. She was most likely on her way back to her clan from her duties at the Blood Watch.

"To think, Oona dead, who had survived so much!" Gwynneth wept over the ragged body of the wolf. Oona's long history fled through her mind. *She marched with the MacNamara expeditionary force, the greatest fighting force in* the Beyond. *She fought in the War of the Ember. And now,* thought Gwynneth, *to be swallowed by the earth, then pecked upon by vultures.* Gwynneth screamed. The sound slammed back at her from the walls of the crevasse as she flew madly about, battering the wind with her wings. It was as if she wanted to punch every god from its heaven, for truly this was hagsmire, hell on earth!

In the midst of the storm that roiled her gizzard, she once again heard the soft mewling of that tiny pup Maudie. *Banja needs food to make milk for her pup.* There was new life in this Glaux-forsaken land and it needed to be sustained. With that thought, Gwynneth pulled herself together. She focused in on a slight scurrying sound and picked off a vole she had seen scampering about. It was owl food, but sustenance nonetheless. Banja would not complain.

"Oh, this is so kind of you, Gwynneth. I can't express my appreciation." Tears now streamed from Banja's old eye and her brand-new one, making Gwynneth think of Edme. Would Edme have a new eye? She was after all a *malcadh* made, not born.

How remarkable. I am looking at Banja and thinking of

Edme! Banja had once been the nastiest wolf at the Ring, and now she evoked thoughts of the kindest.

Gwynneth *wilfed.* Where were Faolan and the Sark? The dear old Sark. *She's hardly the gentlest wolf,* Gwynneth thought, but the Sark had been her first friend in the Beyond.

"Is something wrong, Gwynneth?" Banja paused, then ducked her head in embarrassment. "Well, of course, everything is wrong! How stupid of me. But you suddenly look so sad."

"I was just thinking of my friends — Edme, Faolan . . ." She gulped. "And the Sark."

"You and the Sark were very close, weren't you?"

"Indeed! The Sark and my father, Gwyndor, were the very best of friends. She and my auntie both looked after me at different times in my life. My mother had died and I really never knew her. So when I was very young my auntie took me in, though she was not an egg relation."

"Egg relation — is that what owls call it?"

"Yes, I guess it sounds odd to wolves. And when my auntie was murdered, I went to the Beyond and to the Sark. So I more or less had two foster mothers — an owl and a wolf." She sighed and closed her eyes. "I don't think I could have done any better."

Banja was silent for several moments. When she spoke, her voice was slow, as if she were choosing every word carefully. "Gwynneth." She paused. "If something were to happen to me, would you consider taking care of Maudie?"

"But I'm not a wolf, Banja."

"You know so much about wolves."

"Yes, but not as much as a wolf does. I'm not like Faolan or Edme."

"I was awful to those two wolves when they arrived at the Ring, especially Edme because, well . . ." Banja began to stammer. "She was like me! Missing one eye. I took all my bitterness out on her." She turned her two bright green eyes on Gwynneth. "I'm so ashamed . . . so ashamed I would never dare ask anything of her."

"Of course I'd look after Maudie if something happened to you, but you underestimate Edme. If she's still alive, Maudie would do well by her."

"If you find Edme, perhaps she might, too. Perhaps both of you could look after her together." Banja paused for a split second, then rushed on. "Edme has every right to say no. I was so terrible to her. I wouldn't blame her one bit for telling me to be off to the Dim World."

I think we are in the Dim World. "Dim World" was the wolf term for hell. But Gwynneth held her tongue.

"Knowing Edme, I am sure she would agree to take care of little Maudie, and I will, too."

"Oh, thank you, Gwynneth. Thank you so much." Banja settled back and continued nursing her pup. "Do you know what I think?" Her voice was slow and drowsy. Gwynneth had seen other wolf mums become this way when they nursed their young. The act of giving milk seemed to have a calming effect on them. Banja yawned. "You know what I think?" she persisted.

"What's that, Banja?"

"I think you need to go and look for the Sark — your foster mum."

"You're right," Gwynneth agreed. "But don't worry. I'll be back."

"I won't worry. I trust you, Gwynneth."

Trust? It was a word that Gwynneth thought she would never hear coming from the mouth of the red wolf. Shock stirred her feathers and this gave her away.

"Yes, trust, Gwynneth. Can you believe I said that?" Banja opened her eyes wide now, surprised at herself. "I tell you, feeling a sense of trust is almost better than seeing with two eyes."

CHAPTER ELEVEN

SHATTERED

GWYNNETH SCOURED THE MUD-
dled terrain between her forge and the Shadow Forest,
where she had last seen the Sark. She flew into the countless crevices that cracked the land and yielded the remains
of many dead animals, from wolves to grizzly bears. But so
far she had not found the Sark. With each dead wolf she
encountered, she had to admit she was relieved that it
was not the Sark. Was it possible that the Sark had made
it back to the Slough? With its spongy marshland, the
Slough might not have cracked in the same way the brit-
tle terrain had in the rest of the Beyond. With that
thought in mind, the Masked Owl began flying east by
southeast. But Gwynneth saw nothing, no trace of the
Sark even as she alighted in her friend's encampment.

The kiln, where the Sark had forged her memory
jugs, had collapsed and was nothing more than a heap of

dried mud and the firestones she had collected from the river and used for reinforcing the kiln's foundation. A Slough grouse stalked about with a broken wing, as if trying to survey the damage. And unbeknownst to Gwynneth, inside the winding caverns of her cave, the Sark lay close to death.

The previous evening the Sark had staggered back to her encampment, weak and bleeding profusely. She collapsed just outside her cave and lay there unconscious until dawn. The morning light revived her slightly and she managed to drag herself into her cave only to confront a fresh nightmare. "It can't be . . . it can't be!" she moaned. Every single memory jug was shattered. The Sark felt an answering fracturing in her marrow and crumpled onto a mound of pot shards. To any other creature she would appear nearly dead or deeply comatose, her breathing shallow and irregular. But some part deep within her remained alert.

Was she someplace between earth and the Cave of Souls? she wondered. She felt she was in a different land, a different country, and yet there was a familiar scent she had saved from long ago and put in the jug with the blue glaze. It wafted out to greet her.

That blue glaze was the devil to figure out! She had been explaining to Gwyndor how she had pulled borax from the old salt beds and mixed it with some moose scat. *Oh, forget that,* she told herself. *It's the scent inside the memory jug that's important, not the glaze. It's the scent contained, you crazy old fool!* Her marrow trembled as the first wafts of sweet grass came back to her. *Sweet grass!* Even in her insensible state, her skittish eye began to spin madly.

The odor of the sweet grass swirled up and flooded through her, taking her back to that moon so long ago, when she had just entered her second year. She had been born into the MacNabbys, a small clan with only two packs, but somehow she had lost them. She had not been born a malcadh. *No Obea had come to take her away, she was sure of that. Obeas were said to have no scent because of their sterility, but the Sark had realized very soon how powerful her own sense of smell was. To her, the absence of odor was in an odd way as memorable as the most pungent scent. She would have remembered being carried off to a tummfraw by an Obea. She had therefore surmised that she had been some sort of embarrassment to her parents and had been left behind or*

had been misplaced somehow, accidentally on purpose. Wolf pups, always curious, were known to wander off. Perhaps she had and no one had come to look for her or tried very hard to find her. After all, she had been born very, very ugly.

When, as a yearling, the Sark had discovered a MacNabby pack, she followed them for a while but did not approach. Her fur was mottled and ragged, and her eye had begun to skitter in its socket. The members of the MacNabby clan were exceedingly handsome. She feared that she might not be accepted. It seemed to her better to remain separate. So she had gone off.

Not long after, the Sark caught sight of a MacNabby camp heading back east from the summer hunting grounds. There was a beautiful she-wolf among them with a pelt the color of pale amber, a wolf so stunning that she took the Sark's breath away. The she-wolf was everything that the Sark was not, with well-formed haunches, an elegant muzzle, and the greenest eyes the Sark had ever seen. She was traveling with her mate and three pups, but every male in the pack was excessively attentive to her. More than once, the Sark saw the she-wolf's mate take a nip at her admirers. He was the leader of the pack and it was not simply indecorous that these other males would flirt with their leader's mate, but a violation of the gaddernock, the laws that governed the clans of the Beyond.

The female, whom the Sark called Amber, did little to discourage the other males' flirtatious overtures, which seemed to the Sark another violation of some sort. But what puzzled the Sark the most was how inattentive she was to her new litter of pups. She let them scramble off this way and that and it was always some other pack member who went after them. They were unruly little fellows, all male, and when Amber disciplined them, she was very harsh. More than once, her warning nips drew blood. She was not a good mother; indeed, there did not seem to be a single maternal bone in her body.

Still, she fascinated the Sark. Amber was appallingly vain, so much so that she could hardly pass a lake or a puddle without pausing to stare at her own reflection. She would grow very still, as if her own beauty put her in a trance of some sort.

Then one night, when the pack had stopped by a pond to camp, the Sark had an astounding revelation about who exactly Amber was. The moon was full and the lake looked as if it had been gilded in silver. Not a breath of wind disturbed its surface. It provided the perfect mirror for the beautiful wolf's reflection.

The Sark hid in the grass staring at Amber, wondering why she was so fascinated by the vain wolf. What is it about her? the Sark wondered.

A breeze ruffled the surface, disturbing Amber's image, and one of her pups came up demanding to nurse. Amber snarled, spun around, and gave the pup a sharp whack with her paw. The pup went flying through the air, then hit the ground hard. Just then, the wind changed direction and the Sark picked up Amber's scent for the first time. It was painfully familiar, the scent the Sark had smelled with her first breath of life. This she-wolf was her Milk Giver! This was her own mother.

The pup remained motionless on the ground. The Sark could tell by the angle of its body that his spine had been broken and he was dead. Amber went calmly up to the crumpled body and sniffed it, then picked the little pup up by the scruff of his neck, carried him to the far edge of the lake where the water was the deepest, and dropped him in. There would be no trace of her crime.

So this is my mother! *thought the Sark. And she is a murderer!* The Sark's skittish eye flooded with tears. How can she be this way to her own pup, a beautiful, perfect pup, not a hideous, bobble-eyed, lop-eared pup as I must have been?

She had just witnessed by the bank of the pond an ugliness the Sark could have never imagined. The wolf she called Amber, whom until moments before the Sark thought the *most beautiful wolf she had ever seen, was grotesque. She had an ugliness inside that almost stank, it was so hideous. Her own mother — Amber — was a* malcadh. *Her form was perfect, but her soul was twisted. And for the first time, the Sark realized that although her own body was far from perfect — indeed grotesque — it was just the outside and had nothing to do with what was inside her, the place where her true wolf nature lived. She could not change her form, but she could make sure that her inside never became as deformed as that of her mother. It was perhaps a blessing that the Sark's appearance was slightly monstrous, as no wolf would attempt to mate with her. She dared not pass on her mother's twisted spirit to any pup.*

The Sark watched as Amber stepped back from the water's edge and waited until the ripples retreated from the place she had just dumped her son's body. When the surface was still as glass, she bent her head to observe her reflection for one last time before heading back to the pack.

This was the Sark's strongest sweet-grass memory, one of the earliest she had whispered into a memory jug. And although the blue-glazed jug was broken, there was the whisper of scent from the shards, gurgling up as if from a spring. *How can this be?* she wondered in her strange state. But the shards had reassembled themselves in her mind, pieces of a shattered puzzle that had once again come together. And then the Sark caught the scent of an owl nearby, a familiar owl. *I can smell her. . . . Gwynneth.* Something inside the Sark laughed. *But owls can't smell worth a pile of caribou scat. She'll never find me here with my beloved memory jugs, slipping my pelt at last.*

The Sark was wrong. Gwynneth didn't smell her, but her sharp ears picked up the terrible ragged breathing and she entered the cave. When she saw the Sark, lying in a pool of blood so deep that the shards from her memory jugs almost floated around her, Gwynneth screamed. She screamed as no owl had ever screamed before.

CHAPTER TWELVE

THE OFFING

EDME FELT HER MARROW CURDLE
and little Myrr stopped in his tracks and began to shiver.
"What is that screeching?"

The five wolves had decided to head across the
Slough, determined to find the Sark although their hopes
were dwindling with each dead animal they encountered.
Faolan was desperate. Ever since he had stated with such
certainty that they must go west to the Distant Blue, he
had become deeply apprehensive. What if the blue land
that he had once glimpsed had been some sort of delu-
sion? When he had stood on that cairn on the Blood
Watch, he had been exhausted, weak from hunger, weak
from fighting off vicious outclanners. The Distant Blue
could have been a figment of his imagination, a halluci-
nation brought on by famine. Yet in his marrow, Faolan

felt there was a truth to that looming blue place and it beckoned strongly. The Sark would know for sure. Faolan would find his dear friend, and they could set off for the Distant Blue together. He would never leave her behind, not with the whole of the Beyond broken and dying.

The terrible screeching seared the air again. There was something almost hauntingly familiar about it —

Faolan was seized by sudden fear. "We have to travel fast." He set a pace approaching the press-paw speed of a *byrrgis*. A sense of urgency coursed through him and the others could barely keep up. Poor little Myrr lagged so far behind that Edme turned around and grabbed him by the scruff of his neck the way a she-wolf carries her youngest pups.

This is so embarrassing! Myrr thought as he swung from Edme's jaws. *What would my mum say?* The thought shocked him.

He had not thought of his mum or his da in a while, not since he had been brought to the Ring almost a moon before. He couldn't bear to think of how his parents had turned away that last time. It was as if his parents had stared right through him, and then just turned their backs and walked away. But he remembered them now. Before his parents had gone *cag mag*, his mum used to carry him this way all the time.

I shouldn't think about her, he told himself. *It will only make me sad. Edme is kind, Faolan and his sisters are kind. Don't think about Mum ever, ever! Not even the good memories. We're going west now. Things will be better. We're going west!*

Faolan had climbed up onto one of the few promontories in the Slough. Now he could see that the source of the terrible screaming was, just as he'd feared, an owl. Gwynneth was flying in circles over the Sark's encampment, her head tipped back as she shreed her grief to the sky.

"She is dying, dying! What can I do? I bring her food and she will not wake to eat. I would carry her in my talons to the ends of the earth, but she sleeps on."

Now Faolan understood. The Sark was close to death! Faolan turned to the others and howled the terrible news, "The Sark! The Sark is dying."

Gwynneth lighted down when she saw her friends approaching the encampment. "You're safe! You're here!" She was about to say, "Thank Glaux," but then she remembered she was angry at Glaux and angry at Lupus. "I've tried everything. I killed a wing-lame grouse and tried to squeeze the blood into her mouth. I found some of her ointments for the cut on her flank, b-b-but . . . I can't explain it. The bleeding has almost stopped, and yet I cannot seem to bring her back. She's someplace, someplace where she cannot hear me or see me. She's away."

Faolan and the others followed Gwynneth into the cave.

"Look," Gwynneth whispered. "You can tell that her eye still spins beneath her eyelid, just as it so often does when she's awake."

"She must be seeing things," Mhairie said softly.

"Or smelling things," Faolan replied as he looked about at the thousands of pot fragments. He turned his gaze back to the Sark. The pool of blood around her had dried. "Despite her twirling eye, she seems, well . . . I don't know. At peace."

"Her breathing has eased some, I think," Gwynneth said.

"If we could get her well, we could take her with us," Faolan said.

"Where are you going? Where is there to go?" Gwynneth asked, recalling Banja's words.

"West. We're going west."

"To the Blood Watch?"

"Beyond that," Faolan replied.

"To the Outermost?" Gwynneth asked in a hushed voice.

"Beyond even that."

Gwynneth's beak dropped open. "Faolan, what have you seen?"

CHAPTER THIRTEEN

"No! No, and No Again!"

"NO!"

The five wolves and the owl startled.

"Who said that?" Gwynneth asked.

"Me, you fool." The Sark's eyes slid open. Her pelt had shrunk on her until every bone seemed ready to poke through.

"Oh, dear Sark, we thought we had lost you!" Gwynneth flew up to hover above the Sark's head and waft her with her wings.

"Quit batting your wings around my head," the Sark rasped. Her breath was still and the words came out like the jagged shards of the shattered memory jugs on which she lay.

"You need to rest, get well." Edme edged close to her.

"Yes, Sark, we'll get you some food. There seems to be

more small game about." Faolan approached and kneeled close to her ear.

"Don't get me anything! I have all I need right here." The Sark stirred slightly on the fragments of pottery.

"But those must be uncomfortable," Edme said. "Don't you want us to move you to a pelt? We could find some of the old pelts from your bed, put them under you, and then when you're rested, we'll all head west."

"West?" the Sark asked.

"Yes," Faolan said. "It came to me that —"

But the Sark cut him off.

"I am not going anywhere, nowhere. I'm fine right here. I want no pelts, only my pots shards."

"B-b-but —" Gwynneth protested. "That's impossible! You need to rest, to get better!"

The Sark looked up at Gwynneth, her gaze gentle for once. "Why is it impossible? I am doing the most possible thing."

"You'll die!" Gwynneth wailed.

"Exactly, the most possible thing. I shall die right here, right here. None of you understand, do you, dear creatures?"

They all shook their heads. *Understand, dear creatures?* Now Gwynneth was truly worried, for the Sark never used terms of affection or tenderness and her voice had lost its rasp and become quite tender.

"I am here with my pot shards, on a bed of fractured memories slowly coming back together. This is my heaven, my Cave of Souls." She looked at Gwynneth. "My Glaumora." She reached out with a palsied paw and touched Faolan's shoulder lightly. "And my Ursulana." Her breathing became more labored and her eyes rolled back into her head. She shut them tight and then opened them once more, seemingly startled. Her spinning eye grew still as she framed Gwynneth and Faolan, the only two creatures in the Beyond that she was truly close to. Then she shut her eyes for a final time. A thin filament of wind blew through the cave as the Sark of the Slough passed from this life to the next.

They were all silent for a long time, the wolves erect with their hackles raised, Gwynneth *wilfed* to the slenderness of a sapling branch.

Finally, Faolan spoke. "Let us leave as quietly as possible. Heed where you walk. No shard should be disturbed. Not a one."

As they were leaving, Myrr turned around for one last look. He had heard all about the Sark in his short life.

Wolves feared her and yet many went to her when they were sick. It was said she was a witch of some sort. They said she knew fire and that was wrong, dangerous, a violation of the Great Chain that linked the wolves to the Cave of Souls and to Lupus. Only owls, like Gwynneth, were supposed to know fire.

But Myrr saw that none of the wolves here feared the Sark at all. They knew her in a way others did not. No one in his clan had ever talked of the Sark's memory jugs, and that was what intrigued Myrr the most. What were these jugs and how did they work? The Sark was so bound to them that she chose to lay down on their sharp pieces. What were her exact words? *I am here with my pot shards, on a bed of fractured memories slowly coming back together. This is my heaven, my Cave of Souls, my Glaumora.* But how could that be? Myrr had only wanted to scrub every memory of his parents from his mind. He was determined to forget them. He hated them!

The Sark's chest was absolutely still. Why would she choose to die like this, on this pile of rubble?

"Come along, Myrr," Edme said gently. "And careful not to disturb the shards."

"I don't understand," Myrr said, his voice cracking. "What?"

"These jugs . . . these memories . . ."

Hearing this, Faolan turned around. "That's really all we are, Myrr — memories. Or call them stories. On the outside we look like fur and bone, or owls with feathers and wings and gizzards. But in the end, we're simply stories. Long, long stories."

I want to forget my story!

"Come along, dear, I'll carry you like before if you like," Edme offered.

"No!" Myrr could not let her carry him. It would bring back a memory that would be as sharp and painful as a snow thorn in his paw pads. "I can walk fine."

CHAPTER FOURTEEN

BEYOND THE BEYOND, BEFORE THE BEFORE

THEY HAD BEEN TRAVELING FOR some time in a northwesterly direction, and although the glacier seemed to have missed the Slough entirely, they could now see it quite clearly as they approached its ragged edge. Faolan called a halt. He peered out across the expanse of ice that seemed endless. The glacier did not appear to be moving at all anymore, but the vast stretch of it stood between the wolves and their destination.

"I don't think we have a choice. We're going to have to go across it if we are to get to the border, to the Cave."

"It looks solid," Mhairie said. "I don't see any cracks."

"You never can be sure. It can be deceptive," Gwynneth said. "I spent a fair amount of time in the northern kingdoms as a youngster. Snow can form a crust over the cracks and the crusts break. You can fall into a deep crevasse."

"What's a crevasse?" Myrr asked.

"It's a deep open crack in a glacier. Deep enough to swallow a grizzly." She *wilfed* before their eyes.

"What is it, Gwynneth?" Faolan asked.

"Nothing," she lied. The memory of Oona sprawled in that deep crevasse haunted her. Faolan looked at her narrowly and she sighed. "Look, I didn't want to tell you. But before we met up in the Slough, when I was traveling near Crooked Back Ridge — well, what had been a ridge — the ground was riddled with deep cracks. I found Oona in one."

"Oona!" Edme and Faolan both gasped.

Gwynneth shut her eyes tight as she recalled the image of the vultures diving into the crevasse, scavenging the remains of animals who had plummeted to their deaths. "It was horrible. The crevasse that Oona fell into was wide, wide enough for the wingspan of a vulture. Wide enough for a grizzly. There were so many animals dead at the bottom. It was a feast for carrion eaters."

"Listen, all of you," Faolan said, shaking the image from his mind. "We have to pass this way. There is no choice. But I tell you we are not going to become food for carrion eaters. Gwynneth, you fly out ahead and scout for any crevasses. We shall walk carefully. We've all been taught to walk on river ice, testing it with our dewclaws. We shall do the same here. Do you understand?"

The other wolves nodded solemnly.

Faolan squared his shoulders, raised his tail, and then barked, "Let's go!"

The five wolves set off, Gwynneth flying above to scour the landscape for any dangerous breaches in the ice and listen carefully for any gaps in the wind as it swept over the glacier that might indicate a crack.

This scheme worked for a little while, until a ground fog rolled in and blocked her surveillance. She swooped down to her companions below.

"It's hard to tell what's below from up there. Before this ground fog rolled in it looked fairly clear. However there's something else I need to tell you."

I am so bad at this kind of thing, she thought. There was no gentle way she could introduce the subject that was troubling her. She wished there was the language equivalent of a slipstream, the partial vacuum created in the wake of another larger bird that allowed one to fly swiftly, barely stirring a feather. But there wasn't, so she just blurted out the news.

Edme gasped in dismay. "What? What are you saying, Gwynneth?"

"Banja has a pup. I found her in my old forge." She ruffled her feathers. "I know this sounds strange."

"Definitely!" Faolan said. "It chills me to think of that wolf as a mother."

"Well, that's perhaps the strangest part. She's a very good mother," Gwynneth replied. "It has changed her completely. She's a different wolf."

"To put it mildly," Mhairie sniffed. "She was a Watch wolf who was not supposed to mate, and here she has a pup."

"Yes, she's a mother now. And anyway, I don't think anyone can consider themselves Watch wolves any longer. There is no Ring. There is no ember to be guarded."

"Has she mended?" Edme ask. There was a slight tremor in her voice that no one detected except Faolan. He leaned in closer to her.

"Yes," Gwynneth sighed. "She has a second eye. She didn't even realize it until I pointed it out to her."

"But the pup is fine?" Edme asked.

"Yes. It's female. Banja named her Maud. She's perfect."

"That's really good. I'm happy for her. I really am." Tears glistened in Edme's eye.

Faolan cocked his head and looked at his dear friend. In truth, she was so much more than a friend. Those feelings, those undeniable emotions that had racked him as hard as the turbulent waters of the bight, roiled within him again. He had been absolutely desperate when he had thought she might be hurt, or that he might never see her again. He had been prepared to throw himself into that raging sea and drown right then.

"I promised that I would go back for Banja," Gwynneth continued. "Help her. And now that we know that we are going west . . ."

"You can't leave her alone!" Edme interrupted. "You can't! To think that there is new life after all . . . all this." She swung her head about to take in the devastated landscape that had once been the Beyond.

"Go back, get her," Faolan said. "We'll meet you at the Blood Watch."

"But is there still a Blood Watch?" Gwynneth asked. "The cairns on those mountains . . . what could be left of them?"

Faolan swallowed. "We'll meet you at the Cave Before Time."

"The Cave Before Time?" Edme asked. She and Faolan's two sisters seemed startled. They had all sought refuge in the Cave during a blizzard, and none had forgotten its strange paintings.

"Is that what you call it, Faolan?" Mhairie said.

"That's its true name, I believe," Edme replied, turning to Faolan. The green light of that single eye was so intense it pierced his bones to the marrow.

"Yes," Faolan replied softly. "We might find the Whistler there."

There is so much more than paintings in that cave, Edme thought. *So much more!* Edme sensed that at the Cave their journey west would truly begin. That was where the frost wolf she had glimpsed those long moons ago would meet the wolf she knew as Faolan.

She felt a twinge deep in her marrow, but there was another pain even deeper — one in her hind leg, somewhere between her hip and knee. Her femur? But her legs had always been fine, ready to spring forward in a kill rush, or leap from the top of a cairn at the Ring. She took soaring leaps, especially when she was on guard for Stormfast. There was something about that cairn — the keybone on it gave her purchase like no bone in the other four Watch cairns. Her leaps on Stormfast had given her a reputation for strong hind legs. The last thing she needed now was bone freeze. There were liniments that could ease the pain, but once bone freeze set in, there would be no jumping as before. Of course there was no Ring as before either, so perhaps it did not matter. But she had to stay strong. She had to carry on west, Beyond the Beyond, on to . . . where? She was not sure, but she trusted Faolan. Hadn't she always?

The thought caught her up short. *Haven't I always trusted Faolan?* It was as if Edme's mind reeled back in time. *If there is a Beyond the Beyond, there must be a Before the Before. That's where we are going — somewhere before time.* Suddenly, she was frightened.

Faolan explained to Gwynneth precisely how she could find the Cave Before Time, even if the entire landscape had been disheveled. "The stars don't change, Gwynneth. You fly two points off between the port hind paw of the Little Raccoon and the first claw of the Golden Talons." He pointed to the sky, using all the correct owl names for the constellations. "You'll find it. Remember, two points off the port hind paw and the first claw of the Golden Talons — paw to claw."

"Yes, I'll find it. But . . ."

"But what?" Faolan asked.

"How do you know the owl names so well, Faolan?"

"It's a long, long story, Gwynneth."

Faolan tipped his head and looked at his old friend Gwynneth, his first friend in the Beyond, as she took flight.

Myrr wagged his tail. "Is it a memory, Faolan, or just a story?"

"Is there a difference?" Faolan asked, then ruffed up the pup's pelt and rolled him. "Come now, you need some play. Everything might be a wreck, but when was the last time any of us played tag? Let's stay right here for a while. The fog isn't bad at all and we can see the ice is solid."

"I'm it!" Edme said and began to scamper about.

"Be careful," Faolan called. "Don't move outside this area."

But there was a small explosion of snow and Edme vanished. A frightening howl curled into the air and began to dwindle, as if the sound were being swallowed by the earth as the one-eyed wolf plummeted down a deep gouge in the fangs of the glacier.

CHAPTER FIFTEEN

THE LONG BLUE NIGHT

·

THE CAVE WHERE THE WHISTLER had camped had not been as destroyed as he had first thought. He had gone out and scouted for other wolves and, as far as he could ascertain, not a single Blood Watch wolf had survived the earthquake. What the earth hadn't swallowed or crushed, the glacier had. He had seen it approach, slowing by the hour. It was frightening, but it possessed a terrible beauty, an appalling splendor.

Now another sound threaded through the shambles of the Cave, just scratching noises and then something else.

"Where is that coming from?" the Whistler said aloud. He was still unaccustomed to his new voice. The sound he heard was a terrible plangent keening, as if the very earth were crying in some awful *glaffling*. The

Whistler blinked. Nearby, under the debris of the quake, was a singing rock, and he was certain that it was transmitting the mournful sound.

The singing rocks were composed of minerals of a peculiar structure that resonated sound across long distances. This sound had a low, darkly rich tone that he recognized. His fur bristled. He knew that voice. It was Edme! He tore around the area to try to find a clear path so he could press himself against the singing rock. Finally, he found it. The rock had been dislodged and a small crater was left where it had been anchored. But it had not rolled far and, once he scraped off the dirt and ice, the sound was crisp.

He heard the voices of other wolves as well. Faolan, Dearlea, Mhairie, and one other — a pup! They were all there and it was clear that Edme was in some kind of unspeakable danger, trapped, possibly injured. He pressed his ear closer to the rock.

Edme was perched on a ledge of ice just above a deep crevasse, but of all the animals, she was the calmest. Faolan was nearly hysterical. She had never seen him in such a state.

Somehow she had landed on a small ledge and escaped injury. She had not fallen too far — she couldn't even see the very bottom. For the crevasse was not simply a straight vertical slot into the earth, but appeared to undulate. The ice walls were wavery structures with bends she couldn't see around.

She managed to scramble herself upward a bit and was clinging to another ledge slightly higher than the first, but unfortunately a lot narrower. What frightened her the most was the peculiar blue light that suffused the air. She had looked below just once and seen that the light deepened to a darker and darker blue until it was nearly black. It chilled Edme to her marrow. This was a dead black, not like the night chinked with stars. It was the black of everlasting nothingness.

"We'll figure out something, Edme!" Faolan called. "We'll get you out of there."

She heard Faolan and his sisters beginning to argue. In the background, Myrr was whimpering and Dearlea said something about eagles plunging in to retrieve her.

"Don't be ridiculous!" Edme snapped. "A bird with a wingspan of an eagle could never fly in here. It's narrow, like a slot."

Again, her friends above began to argue.

Edme had great powers of concentration and she simply blocked their endless bickering from her ears. Edme had learned a thing or two about ice in the past year, the year of the deep cold when the summer and spring moons came and went but it always felt like winter. She knew that just as there were dozens of kinds of snow, there were at least as many kinds of ice. She could see that she was in what she thought of as a weeping region. There were large patches of the ice sheets that appeared to be slick with water — melt water. This made it all the more dangerous for her. Trying to climb would be deadly; she was lucky that she hadn't slipped off as it was. She peered intensely at the sheer walls of blue ice, her single eye blinking again and again. But it was only her outer eye blinking. The inner eye that guided her remained steadily open, its gaze hard and bright. Some of the melt water had refrozen and glistened luminously like a lens, revealing a complex network of tiny cracks inches beneath the smooth surface of ice. Could she possibly uncover them, excavate them using her dewclaw, the fifth little claw on her front paw? This claw was totally useless for hunting or protection, but it was good for digging and maybe perfect for scraping out these fissures. If she could dig these cracks out, she would have some purchase points and she could attempt a climb. It was going to be time consuming, but she could do it.

She began quietly. She did not want to tell the others what she was trying until she was sure it could work.

And it did work for a while. She managed to lift herself a good distance up from where she had begun. She found lots of little cracks to dig out and afford her a grip. But then she reached a long smooth section with no cracks at all.

Edme was exhausted. "What's happening?" Faolan called down. "I don't hear you scratching."

"I'm taking a little rest." For the first time she felt like crying. She looked at the walls of ice that had imprisoned her, the glowering blue sheet directly in front of her. She had studied it for hours or so it seemed; she had lost track of time in this ice hell, this blue Dim World. She felt as if she knew the ice sheet better than she knew her own body. She had studied its every crack, no matter how minute. She could see the tiny buried bubbles of air. Some were close to the surface, some much deeper. They bloomed like galaxies in the long blue night of the ice, but they were not stars and this was not the sky. She watched as some of the melt water beside her began to refreeze, knowing it wouldn't help her. She needed to go up, not sideways, up, up, up, up to the sky, up to the earth, up to Faolan.

"Has Gwynneth come back yet?" Edme called out. She had left the day before and ordinarily it would not have taken long to cover the distance, but a pup would complicate the journey. There was at least one thing they were all thankful for: The weather had grown warmer, warmer than it had been in countless moons. It meant they could sleep out right next to the crevasse without fear of freezing.

But the warm weather brought new worries as well. If the ice inside the crevasse melted even faster, would it make Edme's position even more dangerous? As it was she was hanging on by her claws. But if the ledge became even slicker . . . Faolan could not bear to imagine what might happen.

"Have you found any more cracks?" Mhairie called down.

"Don't worry, I will," Edme called back.

She could not let her friends know of her despair. Then they might all give up, give up and leave her. She was not ready to die alone, like the Sark. She had memories, but not enough. *Not yet!*

It was just at this moment a deep, sonorous howl unfurled on the wind. Even Edme could hear it.

The Whistler!

CHAPTER SIXTEEN

OF WOLVES
AND METAL

"WHISTLER, I CAN'T BELIEVE IT! How did you ever find us?"

"The singing rocks."

"The ones near the Blood Watch?"

"The very same. One was overturned by the earthquake, but it seems more resonant than ever."

As do you, Faolan thought. The Whistler's speaking voice was so different. The rasp was gone, yet his howling, which had always been beautiful, seemed even deeper and richer.

"Edme's trapped," Faolan blurted out. "She fell into the crevasse and she was scratching out cracks to get a toehold. She managed to claw her way up quite a bit, but now —" His voice cracked. "I . . . I don't know. We think she's grown tired. She hasn't made any sounds for hours. She is not even answering us." Faolan's voice clutched with despair.

He walked to the edge of the crevasse. "Edme, you're just resting, aren't you?" There was no response. "Edme? Edme, guess what? The Whistler just arrived. We're going to figure something out."

"Look!" Dearlea cried. "Look, it's Gwynneth, she's back!" They all tipped their heads up.

The shadow print of Gwynneth's wings stretched across the icy field. She had a lump of something in her talons.

"Great Lupus, she's carrying a pup!" Faolan cried out. "But where's Banja?"

"Wolves don't fly — well, only this little one," Gwynneth said, setting down gently by the wolves. "Meet Maudie. Her mum should be here by evening."

In the strange blue light of the crevasse, something quickened in Edme. She sensed a new alertness in Faolan's voice. For however long she had been suspended in this blue void, what had depressed her most of all was the absolute despair that had seized Faolan. It was as if the very marrow were leaking from his bones.

She heard Faolan's voice. "I have an idea. When Banja arrives, I think we can do it."

"Do what?" Edme called. These were her first words in many hours. "Do what, Faolan?"

"Oh, Edme." His voice soared with delight. "Edme, we're going to get you out."

"How, Faolan?" she yelled.

"We shall be five wolves when Banja arrives. We can make a chain of wolves — a Great Chain!" he howled.

Mhairie and Dearlea looked at each other with apprehension. Was it sacrilege? A profanity to speak of the Great Chain in such a manner? A chain of wolves? The Great Chain was the bedrock of all the codes and laws of the clan wolves of the Beyond. And Faolan was a gnaw wolf! He should know better than to speak so freely of the Great Chain.

The first inscription gnaw wolves were required to gnaw on a bone was that of the Great Chain, carved in descending order, beginning with Lupus.

Lupus
Star Wolves (the spirits of dead wolves who have
    traveled to the Cave of Souls)
air
ceilidh fyre (lightning)
chieftains (clan leaders)
lords (pack leaders)
skreeleens

byrrgis leaders

captains

lieutenants

sublieutenants

corporals

packers

gnaw wolves

unranked Obeas

owls

other four-legged animals

other birds, except owls

plants

earth

fire

water

Banja arrived at twilight. "Of course, of course, I shall be part of this chain — this Great Chain." Her eyes sparkled.

"Faolan," Mhairie said hesitantly. "Are you sure?"

"Sure of what?" Faolan looked at her sharply.

She glanced at her sister "We . . . we are worried. You are calling this the Great Chain, a chain of wolves. Isn't this a perversion of the Great Chain? Isn't it" — she paused — "blasphemous?"

Faolan looked at his sisters aghast. "What's blasphemous is leaving Edme to die alone!"

"No, no!" Dearlea protested. "That's not what we meant."

Mhairie hastened to agree. "We would never leave Edme! It's just, you know, calling it a Great Chain."

The Whistler stepped forward. "What does it matter what it's called, Mhairie? It's just words."

Faolan struggled briefly with this idea. He was happy that the Whistler had come to his defense, but there was something slightly askew in his logic. It did matter what it was called.

Faolan looked at his sisters. He loved them and he needed them to understand. He leaned in and began to speak.

"Mhairie, Dearlea, listen to me. What Whistler says in one sense is right, or would be right if these were different times. But now words are important. A Great Chain, a new Great Chain, is precisely what I mean. Everything has changed in the Beyond. There is no more Ring, the Sacred Volcanoes have been smashed." He swallowed. "There is no more Fengo, no Watch wolves to guard an ember. The land has been disrupted and so has the order. We have been abandoned, so to speak, on a *tummfraw* — a condition that Whistler, Edme, and myself are more than familiar with. It is time for a new order. A new chain of being." He met their green eyes with his own. "And so let us begin now."

A quiet descended upon all of them. Edme, wrapped in the blue light of the crevasse, felt a quiver in her heart. Tears leaked out of her eye.

Gwynneth now stirred. "Mhairie, Dearlea, you must be absolutely certain. You must put your gizz — rather your marrow — into this. For I am a Rogue smith and I know metals and I know a thing or two about chains, be they made of metal or wolves. Here is what I can say for certain — a chain is only as strong as its weakest link."

CHAPTER SEVENTEEN

THE NEW GREAT CHAIN

THE PREPARATIONS FOR THE CHAIN were meticulous. First, each wolf dug divots for their hind paws to anchor them firmly in the ice. With their front legs they would grasp the hips of the wolf in front of them — all except for Faolan, who was the first "link" in the chain. His forelegs would be free to grab Edme. Banja was at the back of the chain and would be the anchor. From her long years as a Watch wolf springing from the cairns to guard the volcanoes, her legs were the strongest of all the wolves, except for Faolan. In front of Banja was Mhairie. The Whistler came next, then Dearlea, and finally Faolan. Gwynneth was to fly overhead, urging them on and ready to detect any weak links.

"All right, wolves, prepare to dig in!" Gwynneth called out. "Port paw secured?"

"Affirmative!" the five wolves responded.

"Starboard paw secured?"

"Affirmative!"

Each wolf's heartbeat quickened. Each thought, *My paws feel anchored, but are they?* They each dug in a bit deeper with their toes.

"Grasp the wolf in front and confirm grip," Gwynneth commanded.

"Affirmative!"

"Affirmative!"

"Affirmative!"

"Affirmative!" came the calls.

Four wolves answered. Faolan did not, as his paws were ready to grasp Edme. He had never been so frightened in his life. Edme's life was dependent on him, and the four wolves behind him could all perish if the plan failed. They could all plunge into this void of blue ice.

"Engage now!"

With that the wolves grasped more tightly as Faolan lowered down on his belly and slithered toward the lip of the crevasse. The strange blue light engulfed him. He had expected to see Edme immediately, at least the top of her head, but he realized that the walls of the crevasse were rippled with deep waves. And then there were strange flashes, ice shadows that almost blinded him. Never had he felt such a sense of menace as when he stretched deeper to lower himself down the crevasse.

"I'm here, don't worry!" Edme called.

"Why can't I see you?"

"Stretch out just a little bit more," she urged.

"Not yet!" Gwynneth shrieked. "I have to prepare the rest in the chain." She flew back to the rear of the chain. "Attention, everyone. Faolan has to go deeper into the crevasse. You are all performing wonderfully but now you must tighten your grip on the wolf in front of you. There could be pain, there could be blood. But you must all hold tight!"

Each of the four wolves behind Faolan dug in with their paws. Mhairie felt Banja's claws sink deep into her fur, beginning to rip her flesh.

I am bleeding, bleeding for Edme. The tear was like a stone dropping into still water and rippling through the chain of wolves. *For Edme, for Edme, for Edme. We bleed for Edme.*

Faolan hardly felt the flesh tearing in his hips. He had only one thought. If only he could have his old splayed paw back. Though it was misshapen, it was nevertheless bigger and, he imagined, stronger than the new paw. That old paw had condemned him at birth, but he knew it so well. *So well, so well.*

"Don't!" Edme barked. "Don't think about it." The top of her head appeared, then that single green eye. "Don't think about that old paw, Faolan." She was reaching for both his paws. At the moment Edme's paw touched his, Faolan felt Dearlea begin to slip.

CHAPTER EIGHTEEN

BLOOD AND STARS

THERE WAS A TERRIBLE HOWL AND then a shree. Edme felt Faolan's paws jam in the pits where her shoulders met her forelegs. He had good leverage, then two sharper claws seemed to come out of nowhere and sink into her brow. Blood ran down her face but then there was the wonderful sensation of rising. *Up . . . up . . . up . . .* she willed herself straight up. One by one the stars winked and she rose into the blackness of the night and finally flopped onto a snowy mound. "Earth! Earth and sky!" That was all she could say. Faolan was licking the blood from her face. His own hips were bleeding from tears made by Dearlea's claws.

"If it hadn't been for Gwynneth," Faolan gasped, "we would have all fallen into the crevasse."

"Gwynneth?" Edme was confused.

Dearlea began to cry. "I was the weak link."

"Nonsense!" Faolan said. "You did your very best."

"But when I started to slip it was Gwynneth who saved you, Edme. She flew right down into the void and grabbed your head with her talons. She lightened the load so I could dig in again."

"The chain didn't break, Dearlea," Gwynneth said firmly.

"You were the first to slip because you were the first after Faolan," the Whistler said.

"Whistler's right. It could have been any of us. You were the first to feel him take the whole weight of Edme, and if it hadn't been for Gwynneth . . ." Banja didn't finish the thought.

Edme staggered to her feet. She looked around. Five wolves lay in the moonlight, exhausted. The snow was splattered with their blood. "You saved me," she said to them. "You all saved me from a terrible kind of death. With your blood, your muscle." She turned and looked at Gwynneth. "Your wings and your talons. You saved me. I am forever grateful, forever in your debt."

Faolan rose to his feet. His hip had stopped bleeding. "There are no debts. We can't think that way. We must find a den near here. Rest some and then go on. For there is a new place for those who are willing, who are able, who are strong. We are going west. There is, I believe, a new world somewhere waiting. The moon that shines here will shine there, but here the land is broken and there it is whole."

Edme tipped her head to one side as she listened to Faolan. Something shivered in her marrow. *Is it truly a new land or is it an old one? Is it the land of the frost wolf?*

They found the ruins of an old whelping den that was large enough for all of them to squeeze in. However, after what had seemed to Edme like an endless time in the crevasse, she had no inclination to sleep inside a den. She insisted on staying just outside even though it had turned cold again.

"I'll be fine, Faolan. Look, I'll sleep here right at the mouth of the den."

She needed to see the sky, the black night dusted with stars. She needed to feel the wind whisper through her fur. She caught the shadow of Gwynneth's wings printed on the snow.

"You're not sleeping inside with the rest?" Gwynneth asked.

"No. To tell you the truth, I've never been much for dens. Especially not after falling into that crevasse."

"It must have been terrible."

"It was the nothingness of it that I found frightening. The nothingness and the blueness."

"The blueness?"

"Yes, that odd blue light that was always there no matter day or night. It was always the same."

"You were down there for two nights and one day," Gwynneth said.

"It seemed forever, but the light never seemed to change. The color never changed." She paused and blinked her single eye. "I never thought of this before, Gwynneth, but have you ever flown so high that you see only the blueness of the sky and nothing else?"

"Oh, there is always something, even though I might not be able to see the ground. Often I can't see the ground because of clouds. But there is never nothingness and it is never simply blue even on the brightest days. It is like black is never black."

"It isn't?" Edme asked, cocking her head.

"No, never. There is First Black, that's what we call it. We're past that time now and owls would call this the Deep Gray, the time just before the dawn. And then at the opposite end of the day — what you call twilight — there is what we call First Lavender, that begins to move into the Deep Purple that pulls in the First Black." Gwynneth was perched on an upturned chunk of ice.

"Will you go west with us, Gwynneth?" Edme asked.

The Masked Owl *wilfed* and became as slender as a reed.

"I didn't mean to disturb you. I shouldn't have asked," Edme quickly apologized. Owls *wilfed* when they were either frightened or were trying to appear almost invisible while keeping watch for prey.

"It's all right. Don't worry." Gwynneth paused for a long time. "You know, Edme, I've always been somewhat of a loner. Preferred living in the Beyond closer to wolves really than owls. I lost my mum so young that I barely remember her. Then my auntie followed, and not long after my da, and now the Sark. But what am I going to do here, completely alone in an empty land? The herds are gone, so there isn't even enough scat to fuel my fires. I'm not sure what this place is that Faolan is thinking of. It could be nothing, it could be a dream. But I'll go."

"I'm glad. I'm really glad you're coming with us. After all, you were Faolan's very first friend in the Beyond."

"So I was," Gwynneth said.

Edme flinched.

"Is something wrong?" Gwynneth asked.

"No, nothing really. It's just a crick. I couldn't move much on that ledge and my hind legs have stiffened up a bit."

"You should get some rest," Gwynneth said.

"What about yourself?"

"For our kind, sleep is for the day, not the night," the owl replied.

Edme circled three times as if she were in a den before she settled down on the ground. The cold didn't bother her in the least. She felt wrapped in the black pelt of the night and the stars seemed to shine just for her. She wondered if she would ever want to sleep in a den again. She closed her single eye and beat back the horror of the ice walls, of the long blue, and feasted on the night.

As she slept she felt a twinge in her hind leg. *I know this pain, this old pain, but why?* She shifted her position. In her dream, she caught a glimpse of a familiar wolf. *Ah, the frost wolf,* she thought. But no, this wolf was smaller and it limped. Two bright green eyes seemed to stare directly into her eye. *You know me?* the eyes seemed to say. But not a word was spoken.

A furry little ball pressed into Edme's flank and woke her. It was Myrr. She yawned sleepily.

"It's cold out here, Myrr."

"It's warm next to you. I missed you."

"I missed you, too," she mumbled as she slid back into her dream. *But there is something I miss even more.* Once more she felt the pain in her hind leg.

CHAPTER NINETEEN

THE TOE
OF THE GLACIER

FOR THREE DAYS THE SIX WOLVES, two pups, and the Masked Owl traveled together. The ruptured land made for slow going, but there was an amazing amount of small game. It was as if the spasms of the earth had unleashed a torrent of small rodents — voles, mice, and a large population of lemmings scraped up by the unmoored glacier. It was decidedly owl food, but after almost ten moons of famine the wolves learned quickly to adjust. Although they did look askance at Gwynneth's manner of eating — with one quick gulp, the creature vanished headfirst into her beak and down her gullet.

"I just don't understand how you do it," Mhairie said as she watched Gwynneth make quick work of a vole. "I mean, don't you chew at all?"

Gwynneth gave a slight belch, then replied. "No teeth, dear."

"It sounds almost too simple," Dearlea said. "I mean, how can you taste it?"

"It's an aftertaste as the vole begins to break down in my stomachs, my two stomachs. The second stomach, that's our gizzard, and that's where we owls pack away all the fur and bones."

"Eeew!" Myrr said.

"Now, Myrr," Edme scolded gently. "We all have our ways and we must respect each other."

"But when owls are just pups how can they do that?"

"We don't call them pups, Myrr, when they are young. We call them owlets."

"Well, when they are owlets how can their stomachs be big enough for a whole vole?"

"Oh, they're not. We pick the meat off the bones with our talons for owlets to eat. It's called their 'first meat ceremony.' Before that, owlets have only eaten bugs and things — crickets, worms."

Myrr shut his eyes. "I am really trying to be respectful about all this but — eating bugs!"

Faolan looked on. "I used to eat bulbs and roots when I was just a cub. I mean a pup," he said, thinking of Thunderheart.

"You did? Why?"

"It's a long story for another time. Come on. We have

to get on." Faolan was about to say "on the trail." But there were no trails left in the Beyond, no scent posts. It was as if the earthquake had erased everything.

Gwynneth's habit was to fly out ahead to scout the best route west. She had not been flying long when she looked down and saw an inexplicable formation beneath her. "What in the name of Glaux," she whispered to herself. She first saw the dark tracks left by the surge of the glacier — thick deposits of soil and rock that had been peeled from the surrounding earth at the edges of the glacier. She thought again of what the owls in the north called a galloping glacier. Had the gallop stopped here in this peculiar pile of rocks, ice, and trees? A crushed forest seemed to pop out of the debris. And it was not just any forest, but one of the spirit woods that fringed the eastern side of the bight from Broken Talon Point. The toe of the glacier had raced from the northern kingdoms across the Bittersea, and then the Sea of Hoolemere, and through the Beyond on its relentless course to the west. And it had brought with it fragments of its plunder from all the landscapes it had crossed through.

⟩ A *spirit woods!* Gwynneth felt herself begin to *wilf* at the very idea of one of these haunted forests where the scrooms of owls and the *lochins* of wolves often gathered. Her wings stuttered. *Don't you dare go yeep! Don't let your wings lock! You're dead if you do!* But she felt herself begin to plummet.

A vortex of mist swirled up before her eyes. A scroom! Da! She felt her wings unlock and there was a surge in her gizzard. She caught the wind and began to soar as a warm updraft billowed beneath her. She closed her eyes for a split second. *My father's scroom sent this updraft and saved my life.* When she opened her eyes and looked beyond the edge of the rolled forest, she could see a clear path to the farthest western boundary of the Beyond at the Blood Watch. This was the way they must travel if they were to go west. It was as if her father Gwyndor's scroom had commanded — *bring them this way.* There was a reason for her father's scroom to appear at the moment it had. There was a reason for them to travel this way and not the route the Whistler had come.

It was not until moments later, as she still glided down on the warm thermal, that she realized that there had been a bright glint at the very center of the vortex of scroom mist, like a small sun radiant in the dark of this night. *Da's helm!* He was wearing the helm and visor that she had restored to the blue spruce tree.

"I saw the end!" Gwynneth called.

"The end of what?" Edme asked.

"The glacier. I spotted the toe, the toe of the glacier."

"How can that be?" the Whistler asked. "I came this way from the Blood Watch and I didn't see it."

"You came farther south from here. There was thick fog that night. Remember? Maybe you just missed it. We need to go across the toe and . . ." Gwynneth stopped.

"And what?" Faolan asked.

"And into the woods."

"Woods? What woods?" the Whistler asked. "There are few real woods in the Beyond and none near here."

"Yes, I know," Gwynneth answered.

"So what woods?" Mhairie pressed.

"A spirit woods." Gwynneth inhaled and blinked her eyes rapidly. "I'll explain when we get there."

CHAPTER TWENTY

INTO THE SPIRIT WOODS

IT HAD BEEN A LONG TREK ACROSS the glacier, but they finally arrived at the toe.

"Well," Mhairie said as she looked about. "Being a wolf of the Beyond, I haven't seen many forests in my life. But I must say, I never pictured one looking like this!"

The toe of the glacier had dug into the land, kicking up an immense pile of earth and debris. Trees stuck out every which way at odd angles. There were ancient hemlocks and spruce, but the most common were the white-barked birch trees, their slender limbs poking into the ground or clawing at the sky like bones picked clean. Though it was night when they arrived at the toe, the pale eerie whiteness of the birch seemed to hold the darkness at bay. Even the stars looked dusty in this powdered night.

Edme shivered. *I'm not an owl, but I might just* wilf, she thought as she felt her marrow turn cold. She looked at Faolan. He seemed calm yet very alert, as if he were anticipating something. But what might one anticipate in such a place? For Edme the pale forest diluted the dark and she found herself yearning for the blackness of the star-cut night that she had come to treasure since falling into the crevasse.

"Must we stay, Faolan?" she whispered.

"It's all right, Edme. Don't be afraid." He ran his muzzle through the fur on her shoulders. Her hackles were raised and bristling.

"But must we stay?"

"Yes, for a little while. It was a hard trek here. Myrr and Maudie are exhausted. We'll just rest for the night. But I can tell Gwynneth is right. The way is smoother from here on to the west. It's not even a day's run from here to the Cave."

"The Cave Before Time?" Edme tilted her head, and once again the light of that single green eye seemed to bore straight into Faolan. "How do you think it came by its name?"

"I don't know. And yet I have always known that was its name. There are some things like that. You don't learn them, you simply know them. You carry them with you always." He paused, then whispered, "From before time."

"From before your time," Edme said quietly. Faolan blinked.

Once again, Edme felt a twinge in her hind leg. Was this something she had carried with her always, without really being aware of it? She looked about and shivered although it was hardly cold. There was something about the remnants of a far-off spirit woods that was profoundly unsettling to her. She was surrounded by broken trees, some with the sap beginning to leak out from their trunks now that the weather had warmed. In one, a dead seagull was tangled in the white limbs of a toppled birch. The roots of the tree had dropped clots of dirt on its dangling head.

"What's a seagull doing here? We're so far from any sea," she asked.

Gwynneth flew up at that moment. "This spirit wood was near the edge of the Sea of Hoolemere, near the bight. That gull must have gotten caught somehow and blown down in a gust just when the glacier was surging through. Probably didn't know up from down, sky from ground. Went yeep."

Edme closed her eyes. If she were a bird, she was

likely to go yeep in this strange place. "Go along, Edme," Faolan urged. "You're tired."

"There is a good place to sleep over there," Gwynneth said, flipping her head about to indicate an enormous tree that had been uprooted, leaving a huge denlike cavity beneath it. "The little ones are already settling down."

"Are you going to sleep out again, Edme?" Faolan asked.

— She was tempted to say that it was difficult to tell "in" from "out" in such a place. Another dead bird was hanging precariously from a branch, this one a little sparrow of some kind. It was as if this forest had scooped up the last scraps of life and caught them in midflight. This strange, churned-up land seemed a sepulchre for death, for bones.

Edme cast a glance toward the dusty sky. "Yes, I suppose I'll sleep out."

Gwynneth gave a little shiver and *wilfed* slightly.

"I think I'll sleep in with the others."

Faolan and Edme both looked at her. "But it's night!" Faolan said. "You always fly at night. Owls sleep in the day."

"Yes, but it's hard to tell day from night here, isn't it?" She paused. "Can't tell twixt from tween time."

"I always get confused. Which is which?" Edme asked.

"Twixt is just when the last of the old gray of the night vanishes and the first drop of light from a new dawn rises. Tween time is the last drop of the Deep Purple and the first drop of the Black."

Gwynneth's feathers ruffled slightly, as if some spectral wind had passed through them. But there was no wind. She resisted telling them all that she knew about the spirit woods. Wolves were superstitious enough as it was. She knew that in their eyes owls were predominantly rational creatures. It would not do for her to blather on about scrooms and such. She especially did not want to disclose anything about the spirit of her father, Gwyndor, materializing. She found it very odd that he had spoken to her not in the vague language and oblique manner of most scrooms, but in a crisp and clear voice. Indeed he had charged her with leading the wolves to the west by way of the misplaced spirit woods. How could she explain all this? Better not discuss it at all.

Gwynneth looked about and realized that the spirit woods contained fragments of other trees. Hemlock, spruce — silver spruce that only grew on the island in the Bittersea, the isle where the Great King Hoole had hatched out under the watchful eye of Grank. It was as if the glacier had rolled in all sorts of slivers of the Hoolian empire. She had a peculiar feeling that this glacier, torn loose by the earthquake, had some sort of conscious mind. As if it wanted to take relics of an old world with it on its march across the Beyond.

Edme was having a very difficult time settling in. Unlike Gwynneth, she had no desire to sleep inside with the other wolves. At first, she settled under a snarl of broken birch limbs that framed the rising constellations in the east. But she could not sleep, and the ghostly white branches made her feel as if she were in a cage of bones. She rose and found another spot, finally curling up for the remainder of the night. She could see the first rungs of the star ladder rising in the east. But all the constellations appeared dim, as if they were made from dust.

Faolan slept out as well, and in his dreams he caught glimpses of rags of mist that seemed to swirl through this topsy-turvy forest like the fitful wraiths of creatures past. *Am I molting?* he wondered as a new lightness engulfed him and he climbed deeper into the powdered night of his sleep.

Fionula the gadfeather hovered briefly over the sleeping form beneath her. She began to sing a soft ancient song from the northern kingdoms. The music unfurled from her throat and she cocked her head to better see the silver wolf. She spotted the spiraling pattern on Faolan's paw. Even though the paw was no longer splayed, the whorled markings on the pads remained and the meaning became clear.

Gyre *souls we are!*

Finally, Faolan understood the meaning of that word, *gyre.* There was a coming and going of his being, of lives through the centuries — a time of disintegration and assembling. In every end a beginning, and in every beginning an end — a cycling that was infinite, a spiraling as old as the constellations sliding through the night skies.

The gadfeather from another time and the wolf in the fractured land seemed to move together through this spirit wood like visitors to a strange land. Soon an immense shape loomed beside them. The sound of its beating heart shook the trees of the woods. *Eo?* Faolan thought, turning to the bear. Eo nodded.

Time to go west, Fionula? thought Eo. Fionula nodded, spinning her head around almost completely so she could look at Faolan.

At that moment Edme stirred in her sleep. Opening her eye she saw three figures — an owl, a bear, and a wolf.

Are they real or lochin? And was the wolf Faolan or the frost wolf? A luminous but tattered pelt hung on the wolf's thin body, a body that belonged to an ancient wolf.

Who is that? He's so old but with the gait of a young wolf — a wolf caught in between. Edme felt a shiver pass through her marrow.

The wolf turned and looked at her for just a moment. He seemed such a paltry thing, so fragile. He was saying something, his voice muffled and yet the meaning clear.

This is no country for old wolves. Our time is almost finished. . . . .

But the dead forest swallowed his words and Edme could not hear the rest.

CHAPTER TWENTY-ONE

THE WIND OF
HER WINGS

"NO, NO!" EDME WAS WRITHING in her sleep.

"Wake up, Edme! Wake up!" Faolan batted her with his muzzle. "You're having a bad dream. Wake up!"

Edme's eye blinked open. "Faolan! It's you."

"Yes, of course. Who else?"

"You're all right?"

"I'm fine. You must have been dreaming."

"It was a terrible dream," Edme gasped. "You were old and weak and . . . and . . ."

Faolan felt a twinge in his marrow. There was no way she could have seen what had happened last night, his walk through the spirit woods. If she had seen something, she might have thought it was *lochin* or scrooms. But Eo and Fionula were not ghosts, they were his *gyre* souls, his brethren through time, through centuries. And he had felt another presence beside him last night. Had Edme glimpsed that soul with her piercing single eye? Was it the old wolf she had seen in her dream?

Faolan pressed hard on his paw and looked down at the print it made. The spiraling marks were left in the snow. Faolan had spent his entire life perfecting his gait so that his track would not be visible. But the spiral mark was the last remnant of the paw that had declared him a *malcadh*, and now he valued it because it signified something much greater.

The other wolves were just coming out from the den under the upturned tree. Gwynneth had assumed a perch on the stump of a silver spruce. She looked refreshed from her rare night of sleep, and spread her wings as if to air them out from a night spent inside and not flying abroad. "Our course is due west," she said. "Few of the familiar landmarks are left, so keep the rising sun on your tails. There's not much cloud cover today and I'll fly low so you can see me. As we draw closer, perhaps Whistler can take the lead, for the terrain may be more familiar to him than to me. We're close to the Blood Watch and the border."

The Whistler stepped forward. "Every single cairn used by the Blood Watch has fallen. There are no borders now to speak of."

"But what about the outclanners? Can they just run about willy-nilly now?" Mhairie asked.

"I suppose so — if they're still alive. The few I've seen were dead or severely wounded — legs broken in the quake, heads crushed under tumbling boulders. Indeed, if there is one blessing of these terrible times, it's that our enemies have been vanquished or nearly vanquished. In any case, 'borders' is a useless term, a thing of the past."

A thing of the past. And this pain in my leg, Edme thought. *Is that also a relic of some injury of old?* The ache in her hind leg seemed familiar. It was not unbearable by any means and if she paid attention to how she walked it didn't bother her at all. In fact, she rather liked her new style of walking. Her stride had become longer and a bit smoother. Almost like an outflanker's tread. She noticed that Faolan, too, was walking differently. Perhaps it was just his new paw, but they had been traveling together for some days and this was the first time she noticed it.

She was looking down and concentrating so hard on her walking that she didn't notice that a fog bank had begun to roll in. She looked up, hoping to spot Gwynneth, but a woolly ceiling had dropped down from the sky and within a matter of seconds, it was so thick that she could barely see her own paws. Nor could she hear the reassuring *tupp tupp* of wolf paws hitting the ground around her. Every single wolf had stopped in its tracks. It was as if the powdery light of the spirit woods had clung to them and thickened to an impenetrable whiteness.

"Myrr! Myrrglosch!" she called out frantically. Had the little pup been swallowed by the fog?

"Maudie!" Banja shrieked. A little yip was heard in response.

"Thank Lupus!" the red wolf cried. Edme could hear Banja clamping her jaws on the soft fur of the little pup's neck. But where was Myrr?

"Myrr! Myrr!"

"Don't panic," Faolan called out into the white blankness.

"Don't panic! What do you mean?" Edme barked.

"Everyone stay calm and stay exactly where you are," Faolan ordered.

"Where's Gwynneth?" Mhairie said.

"Here!" The single word peeled through the fog. "All of you do as Faolan says. I'm going to take a roll call. Then I can get a fix on your location."

Gwynneth had been stunned by how quickly the thick fog had blotted out the landscape and swallowed the wolves. Visual navigation was completely impossible. She would have to rely entirely on ear-slit location navigation and the first thing to establish was where each wolf was.

"Faolan!" she cried out.

"Here!"

"Edme!"

"Here!"

"Myrr!" There was only silence.

"Myrr?" Edme's voice broke.

"Myrrglosch!" Gwynneth shreed this time, but still nothing.

Banja, Mhairie, Dearlea, and the Whistler all responded, "Here."

"Where is he?" Edme howled now. "We can't leave. I won't leave!"

"Of course we won't leave," Faolan replied. "We go together. Gwynneth, is there anything you can do?"

Gwynneth felt her gizzard clench. It was up to her now. She had to think fast.

She needed the wolves to gather together in one place but she dared not let them try to find their own way to a central spot. The last thing she needed was for them to go wandering off on their own and fall into a fissure. From their answers to the roll call, she ascertained that the Whistler seemed to be in a fairly protected place. If a gale came up, they would need shelter. She would lead them one by one to the Whistler.

"Whistler!" she called.

"I'm here."

"I'm going to lead the others to you one by one. Nobody move until I set down directly in front of you."

"But what about Myrr?" Edme cried out.

"I shall find Myrr. If I can find a mouse by the beat of its heart from half a league in the air, I can find Myrr. We'll do this quickly and in order. Edme, you're first." It had to be Edme, for as practical as the she-wolf was, Gwynneth sensed she was quivering to dash off into the fog in search of Myrr.

Seconds later, Gwynneth alighted in front of Edme. "Come with me."

"How? I can't fly."

"Of course you can't," Gwynneth snapped. "I am going to fly just above your head. You can feel, can't you?"

"Feel?"

"Feel the wind from my wings." She waved them vig-orously, sending up a small swirl of snow from the ground.

"Yes, I can feel that," Edme said. "But what about Myrr?"

"I shall find Myrr, and when I do I want you here and not lost out there wandering about like some . . ." She paused. "Never mind."

"Idiot. I know. I love the little pup. You don't understand. He lost his parents and now . . ."

"No, Edme, you don't understand. He didn't lose them. They lost him. They turned away from their own son. I was there when they walked away from him. He was begging them. Remember what he said, Edme?"

And the one-eyed wolf did remember. Myrr's words came back to her. *Mum, Da, that's just a wolf, not a prophet . . . just a wolf.* But his parents simply walked away from him. It was Faolan who picked him up in his mouth. The pup had come with them, and Edme had become not his second Milk Giver, for he had been weaned and she had no milk, but his *taiga*, which was as close to being a mother as any Watch wolf could ever really become — until Banja, who broke all the rules of the Ring of Sacred Volcanoes.

It did not take Gwynneth long to lead the other wolves to the Whistler. The fog had become completely impenetrable.

"I just don't understand how Myrr could have so quickly disappeared. He was right behind me and then just gone. He couldn't have fallen into a crevasse, at least I don't think so. I mean, there aren't any around here, are there?"

"No, none," Gwynneth said firmly. "I would have spotted them before the fog came in. Try to stay calm. I am going to fly a scanning pattern."

Gwynneth spread her wings and waited several seconds before lofting herself into flight. During those seconds she tipped her head one way, then another. Finally, she flipped her head almost upside down and backward.

"I'll never get used to that thing they do with their heads," the Whistler whispered as Gwynneth dissolved into the fog. "Makes me a tad queasy."

"I wish the Sark were here," Edme moaned. "Between the two of them, with her sniffer and Gwynneth's ear slits, they would find Myrr."

Banja came up to Edme and ran her muzzle through Edme's withers. "I'm sorry, Edme. I can see how you love that pup. From the first time Myrr arrived at the Ring you were so . . . so . . ." Her voice dwindled. "Tender." The word was barely a whisper. "I never really knew about those feelings until I had Maudie. I'm sorry for so much, Edme." She gulped a bit and continued. "It seems almost wrong that I have so much now. Two eyes and a pup of my own. I don't deserve it."

"Don't talk that way. It's not a question of who deserves what. You are a very different wolf now. With your two eyes and your little Maudie you will do well in this . . . this . . ." Edme turned to Faolan, whose own eyes had filled with tears. "In this new place we are going in the far west."

The far west. The words had a deep resonance that made the wolves' marrow quiver.

Faolan spoke up in a strong clear voice. "Don't worry. No one is going to be left behind, especially Myrrglosch. Remember what his name means — a bit of a miracle."

CHAPTER TWENTY-TWO

BITS OF MIRACLES

A BIT OF A MIRACLE. THE WORDS ran through Gwynneth's head. *That's exactly what I need right now!* she thought. She was picking up scraps of the wolves' conversation on the ground but unfortunately no pup sounds were coming through. The Masked Owl swung her head slowly from one side to another as she flew in ever-widening scanning circles, searching for the distinctive *tip tip* of small wolf paws that was slightly different from the *tupp tupp* of full-grown wolves. The snow-covered ground below was laced with the pitter of scurrying rodents and their rapid heartbeats. There was also the scratching sound of a grouse chick trying to peck its way out of an egg.

Why now? Gwynneth wondered. Grouse didn't hatch out until the late spring moons, but of course the seasons were as tangled as everything else in the Beyond. A jumbled mess. She didn't hear the heartbeat of any parent grouse. The hatchling would die within hours. There was a marmot stalking nearby and Gwynneth knew it would make quick work of the chick. She picked up marmots, grouse chicks, snow squirrels, and snow hares, but no wolf pup.

Then she heard a new sound, something halfway between a whimper and a rumble. It took a broad chest to make such a full-bodied, reverberant sound, but it seemed too high-pitched to be fully mature. *I know that sound,* Gwynneth thought. And it was coming from not one chest but two — two sobbing bear cubs. The sobs camouflaged another sound — a familiar heartbeat. "Myrr!" she hooted as she plunged through the fog.

Fragments of Myrr's speech seemed to fly out on their own wings. He was trying to console the cubs. "I'm alone, too. My mum and da . . . well, they . . . and now . . . Oh dear, Gwynneth!"

"Myrrglosch, the wolves are frantic. You disappeared! Edme is about to —"

One of the sobbing cubs looked up. "Edme?" His great shining eyes glistened. "You said Edme? Edme, the one-eyed wolf?"

"Yes," Gwynneth said. She took a step closer to the little cub. "Great Glaux. You're the cub — the cub that was nearly the cause of the war in the Darklands, the Black Glass Desert."

"Edme saved me!" the cub said. "She saved me and brought me back to my mum and my brother, Burney, here." The words came rushing out of the cub. "And now our mum is gone! Ever since the quake and . . . and . . ." Both cubs were sobbing now.

"I told them that I'm an orphan, too," Myrr began to speak.

"Don't say that word!" the cub named Burney screamed.

"I'm sorry!"

"She's not dead. She's not!"

Gwynneth stepped forward. "Now, stop this quarreling. It will get you nowhere. First of all, what are your names? You're Burney?"

"Yes." The cub nodded.

"And you must be Toby?"

"How did you know that?" said the other cub, who was somewhat darker and slightly smaller.

"You're not exactly unknown. You almost started a war in the Beyond, the first ever between the wolves and the bears." Toby nodded. "You've become separated from your mum?"

"Yes. That's it," said Toby. "We're NOT orphans."

"Did you lose her during this fog? That's how we lost Myrr here."

The two cubs looked at each other, then at the ground. "No, it was before that," Burney said in a small voice.

"It was right after the quake. She just disappeared," Toby offered.

"So that was a while ago and you have been looking for her ever since?" Gwynneth said.

Both cubs nodded, staring at their feet. Gwynneth knew where the bears came from near the river, and she also knew that this was a region where the glacier had been riddled with cracks — wide crevasses that could have easily swallowed a full-grown grizzly. She had seen a dead grizzly in one of the crevasses not far from where Oona had fallen. Gwynneth didn't think it was the cubs' mother, but then again, it could have been.

Gwynneth turned to Myrr. "Myrr, please explain how you found Toby and Burney."

"Well." The pup cocked his head. "I know I'll probably get into trouble for this. But I had just wandered away, just a teensy-weensy bit away because I thought I saw a snow hare. I've never killed a snow hare. I've never killed anything, for that matter. I wanted to prove to Edme I could hunt." The pup frowned. "I wasn't that far away when all of a sudden the fog came in. I couldn't see anything! And I think I would have found my way back, but I hit this patch of ice and started to skid down a pretty steep slope. When I got to the bottom I . . . I . . . don't know. I was sort of all mixed up and couldn't figure out which way to go. I tried going up but it was pretty slippery so I thought well, I'll just walk along the bottom for a while. This is where I came out and I found Toby and Burney. They were, uh . . . crying, and well, I just knew right away that . . . uh, they were sort of like me. Sort of missing."

"All right, that's enough for now. I think I know what we need to do."

"We need to find our mum!" Toby broke in.

Gwynneth nodded. "Yes, of course. We need to find your mum, but don't you think that if you would come with us, six wolves, two pups, and myself — all of us very good trackers — you'd have more of a chance of finding her?"

"Will you really look for her?" Burney asked.

Gwynneth hesitated before answering. She wanted to be truthful.

"Our plan is to head west. That's where we think there is the best chance of surviving. The Beyond is destroyed."

"We can't go anywhere without our mum," Toby replied.

"She's looking for us," Burney said.

"Yes, yes, of course, dear. But your mum might be thinking the same way that we are. That the best chance for surviving now is to go west."

"You think so?" Toby asked.

"I am sure. So come with us. I can lead you back to where the other wolves are waiting for us. You can see Edme again!"

"That would be nice," Toby said. "But she's not Mum."

"Nobody can be your mum except your mum." Gwynneth came up and stroked the cubs' shoulders with her wing. "We know that. But please come along now."

The fog had almost cleared when Gwynneth arrived with the pup and the two cubs.

"Myrr! Myrrglosch!" Edme barked and hurled herself toward the pup. Myrr buried his face in Edme's withers.

"Don't make a fuss, Edme," Myrr whispered. "Look who else is here." He tipped her head toward the cubs. "They need you, too."

Edme disentangled herself. The single eye opened wide. "Toby! Toby and Burney! I can't believe it."

"Bits of a miracle, I think they are," Gwynneth whispered to Faolan.

CHAPTER TWENTY-THREE

BRONKA

—ALL NIGHT LONG THE CUBS WHIM-
pered and called out in their sleep for their mum. Edme
finally got up and nudged Faolan with her muzzle. "Wake
up! Wake up, Faolan!"

How could he sleep so soundly? she wondered. Hearing those cubs crying was torturing Edme. Banja was awake,
her two green eyes glistening in the night.

"It's the saddest thing I ever heard," the red wolf said as
Maudie nursed contentedly. "We've got to go look for her."

"I know!" Edme almost sobbed.

"What? What? What is it?" Faolan sprang to his feet.
He was suddenly fully alert. "Who's crying?"

"The cubs!" Edme and Banja both said at once, their
voices tinged with a huff of disbelief.

"Who do you think?" Edme said. "Look, Faolan, we
have to go out and look for their mum. If it slows us down,

it slows us down. But I won't be able to look into those sad brown eyes if we don't try. And that's that!" She pawed the ground with her foot for emphasis.

"Of course," Faolan agreed. He paused a moment and shook his head as if to clear it. "Banja and Dearlea should stay behind with Maudie and Myrr. You, me, Whistler, and Mhairie can go out. We'll have two teams of two wolves each, with Gwynneth for air surveillance."

The four wolves and the owl set out just as dawn was breaking. The joy with which the cubs had greeted the news that a search for their mum would begin was heartbreaking. No matter how much Faolan and Edme cautioned them not to hope for too much, it was of no use. The cubs were sure that the four wolves and the Masked Owl would find their mum.

The search team backtracked to the place where Myrr had first encountered the cubs.

"I think we have to trace that gully where I found Myrr with the cubs," Gwynneth said. "I didn't take the time to explore it once I had found them, but I think it's a wandering defile and leads into a bigger gorge. There's a branch of the river there, and Bronka might have gone looking for her cubs near a fish hole."

The two teams of wolves split at a fork in the defile, with Faolan and Edme following one branch and Mhairie and the Whistler another. Gwynneth flew ahead to where the two branches rejoined in a wider gorge. The rock walls were so steep that the entire gorge was cast in shadows despite the bright morning sun. But Gwynneth didn't need her eyes. It was her ears that caught the beat of a slowing heart.

➤ *Thump* . . . . *thump* . . . .
. . . . *thump.* The intervals between heartbeats lengthened until she thought each beat might be the last. Gwynneth folded her wings against her side and plunged down through a latticework of shadow and pale sunlight. A huge mound rose up like a mountain in the stream. Blood and chunks of raw meat that had been torn from the bear's body lay on patches of snow on the creek's banks. Gwynneth gasped. Only a rout of outclanners could have done this. Vultures could never tear flesh in that way — in such huge chunks and never from a creature whose heart still beat!

Gwynneth alighted by the immense head of the bear. It was most definitely Bronka, the mum of Toby and Burney. Gwynneth had seen her once before, on that night on the Black Glass Desert before the war with the bears. She would never forget Bronka's roar of joy when her kidnapped son was returned to her, and now this! The great mother grizzly lay dying. Gasping for air, her eyes rolled back in her head.

"Great Glaux!" murmured the Masked Owl. Wolves had done this to her. But how? It was unimaginable that even a full pack of wolves could bring down a grizzly. But perhaps this time it wasn't completely impossible. Bronka was painfully thin and Gwynneth noticed that her hind paw was turned backward at a peculiar angle. She blinked. Something white poked through — bone! Bronka's ankle had broken and a splinter of bone pierced through the thick skin.

A terrible sound rattled out of Bronka's chest and blood began to ooze from her mouth.

Gwynneth bent down low and, pressing her beak to the grizzly's ear, began to whisper. "Listen to me, Great Bear Mother. Listen closely. Your cubs are safe. They are with Faolan and Edme, the wolves who rescued Toby. They are safe, do you hear me?" She paused. Had Bronka's heart stopped? But then she heard another beat. "Safe, your cubs are safe! Great Ursus speed you to Ursulana!" Gwynneth waited and waited and waited, but the great heart never beat again. The grizzly Bronka was gone.

Gwynneth stayed with her for a long spell. She was not sure why. Perhaps it was only to guard Bronka from the scavengers that would show up sooner or later. Perhaps it was to give her soul time to travel on toward Ursulana in peace.

— Soon, however she caught the footsteps of her four companions entering the gorge.

The Whistler gasped. "She was brought down by outclanners, but how?"

"Her ankle, it's broken," Gwynneth explained. "They must have chased her until she collapsed, and then attacked."

The Whistler began sniffing around the carcass and then the tracks that the outclanners had left.

"It's not any rout I recognize. They must have ventured a fair distance from the border to come here."

"I would guess," Gwynneth said.

"What are we going to do?" Mhairie asked. "The cubs won't believe us. They'll want to come and see her, and it's just too awful."

"No!" Faolan said firmly. "We can't allow that." He paused and thought for a second. "We'll do a scent roll."

Of course, Edme thought. What else could they bring back that would be meaningful to the cubs and at the same time prove that their mother was gone to Ursulana?

And so each wolf slowly approached the bear and pressed one side of its face and then its chest against

Bronka's thick pelt of fur. Gwynneth looked on. Normally, wolves scent-rolled in order to disguise their own odor when they set out on a *byrrgis* to hunt. Since she herself had such a poor sense of smell, she felt it would be inappropriate for her to engage in this ritual. She had no pelt. Besides that, how did a bird roll? As Gwynneth watched them, the wolves' eyes began to stream with tears, and she felt an urge spring up inside her. They were experiencing a profound grief that was not just for the loss of the grizzly but for the cubs who had lost their mother. There was so much to mourn in this land and yet so few creatures left to do the mourning. Somehow this terrible passage in the long history of the Beyond must be marked, remembered. To stand at the edge of grief and not mourn with the survivors seemed wrong to Gwynneth. None of them could make jugs as the Sark had to hold her memories, but if a memory could be kept vital, that was important. What difference did it make if she could not smell? The important thing was that Toby and Burney could.

Gwynneth spread her wings and lifted into a very low flight. Once, twice, three times, she flew over the hulking body of the mother grizzly. She kept going back and forth, lowering her wings with each pass so that the feathertips of her primaries brushed the pelt of the bear. The oil of the bear seeped through the downy plummels that fringed the leading edge of her secondary and primary feathers right up to her covert feathers. Soon she was as redolent with the scent of the grizzly as the four wolves.

A wind drifted across the encampment where Toby and Burney had stayed under the watchful eyes of Banja and Dearlea.

"They found her! They found —!" Burney leaped up.

Toby, who had been snoozing, was suddenly alert. He stood up quivering. "It's Mum."

Banja and Dearlea exchanged nervous glances. They, too, could pick up the scent of bear, but not the heavy footstep. Grizzlies made noise when they walked. But before they could stop the two cubs, they were scampering down the trail. They skidded to a halt when they saw the four wolves, and Gwynneth hovering a short distance above.

"Where is she?" Toby shouted. "What have you done with our mother?"

"She's here!" Burney screamed. "I smell her. I know how my mum smells," but his voice began to dwindle.

Edme walked up to the two cubs. Gwynneth lighted down beside her. The smell of the mother grizzly suffused the air. The two cubs started to shake uncontrollably. "Toby, Burney," Edme began, "we found your mother. Gwynneth actually found her, but . . ."

"Don't say it!" Toby shouted. The two cubs covered their eyes with their paws. "Don't say it." It was as if the words were not spoken, the death would be undone. She would live. Time would reverse. Everything would be made right again as long as the words were not uttered.

Gwynneth stepped closer to them. In a small voice meant just for them she said, "When I found her, she was still alive. She was breathing, but she was unconscious, not really aware of anything around her. I don't think she was in any terrible pain. The pain part, the scary part was over. But I did whisper in her ear. And even though she was unconscious, I think she knew what I was saying."

"What did you whisper?" Toby asked in a tiny, almost strangled voice.

"I told her that you were safe. That you would always be safe and that Faolan, Edme, the Whistler, Mhairie, Dearlea, Banja, Myrr, and even little Maudie, and I would take care of you."

"But Maudie and Myrr are so little. How can they take care of us?"

"They can be your friends, can't they?" Edme asked.

The cubs nodded. "But you're a wolf," Burney said. "And so are the rest, and Gwynneth is an owl. You can't be our mum!"

"Of course we can't," Edme replied softly. "No one can be your mum except your mum. But we can love you, watch out for you, and keep you as safe as if you were our own pups."

"You smell just like her." Toby pressed his nose into Edme's withers. Big tears rolled down from his eyes.

Gwynneth had to blink back her own tears. She suddenly swiveled her head around and plucked two covert feathers from her back.

"Here!" she said. "One for each of you."

"To keep?" they both asked at once.

"Of course to keep. You'll always have her scent near you. Tuck them into those burrs between your shoulders."

"But didn't it hurt to pluck your feathers out?" Toby asked.

"Just a little bit. Wear them and remember your mum."

CHAPTER TWENTY-FOUR

THIS VIEW OF LIFE!

ORDINARILY, THE RIDGE FROM
which the Blood Watch commanded its vigil could be
seen from leagues away. It was a rocky profile that reared
up like the jagged spine of some primeval beast, casting
long sharp shadows across the high plains. But the spine
had been fractured and the plains seemed to spread end-
lessly into the savage country known as the Outermost.
The little brigade of motley animals — six wolves, two
wolf pups, two bear cubs, and a Masked Owl flying overhead as scout, made their way to the west.

With the sun just past noon, their shadow prints on
the snow began to lengthen. The design of their silhou-
ettes sliding across one another on the white blanket of
snow was stunning. Occasionally, Gwynneth gave a quick
spin of her head to take it in. It was, she realized, a kind

of chain. She remembered what Faolan had said about the Great Chain — how they needed a new Great Chain — when they rescued Edme from the crevasse.

Everything has changed in the Beyond. There is no more Ring, the Sacred Volcanoes have been smashed. There is no more Fengo, no Watch wolves to guard an ember. The land has been disrupted and so has the order. Gwynneth looked down at the dark shadows gliding across the white snow — the two rotund bear cubs, the tiny wolf pups, the wolves, and her own broad wingspan. The design could make a beautiful chain. If she ever had the good luck to set up another forge, what a challenge it would be to make a piece with such wondrous shapes.

— Gwynneth felt a calm steal into her gizzard. There was a grandeur in this view, this design of these creatures moving away together from famine and death to seek new life on a new piece of earth. How magnificent these different creatures were that must have had life originally breathed into them by one creator, whether it be called Lupus or Glaux or Ursus. How many forms grew out of something so simple.

It took Gwynneth back to those days at the forge in the Beyond when she would devote endless hours to making art pieces. The strong rocks, as the Rogue smiths called those stones and bits of stones that were full of the metals that they used for their smithing, were plentiful in the region where she had set up her forge. They seemed to cry out to be made into something beautiful, not merely weapons. Besides, most weapons were actually rather boring to make — the battle claws, the blades, the helmets — one could only vary their shapes so much. It might be challenging to make double-action retractable battle claws, but once you had done it a few times, it became rather tedious. Gwynneth's preference for making art worried her father, Gwyndor, who had been known for his superb double-action retractable battle claws. But her auntie, the Rogue smith of Silverveil, had forged many items beyond the practical or those made for military purposes.

As Gwynneth looked down and saw Faolan's silhouette stretched out to an immense length across the snow, she remembered when she had first met him. She had been trying to forge a metal replica of a willow leaf. This might have seemed odd to some, as there was not a willow tree nor a willow leaf to be found in the barren landscape of the Beyond. Gwynneth could barely remember ever seeing a willow tree, even in Silverveil where she had spent much of her youth. Where had she gotten such an idea? she wondered.

And where had Faolan gotten this idea about heading west? Certainly he had not experienced a scroomly visit from her dead father, Gwyndor. Had a *lochin* come to Faolan and told him to go west? Whatever the reason, Faolan was now a wolf with a purpose.

She watched as he set a steady pace, cocking his head slightly to starboard as a northwest wind blew across the high plains. He was a magnificent wolf. Huge. His silvery coat seemed to sparkle in the sun. When he waved his tail to indicate a slight course correction, it flashed like a comet streaking down to earth. His gait had altered slightly since his paw mended. She noticed that he bore down heavily on it every few strides, leaving a blazoned mark in the snow as if to declare unequivocally, *A wolf named Faolan has passed this way!*

But why, Gwynneth wondered, did Faolan still have the spiral mark on his paw pad? Banja's second eye had been restored perfectly; the Whistler's twisted throat had straightened and the hole repaired, patched so there was no longer the sibilant hiss when he spoke. Faolan's paw, too, had mended. It was like any other normal wolf's paw except in this one respect. Why was the spiral left? There must be a reason.

The shadows on the ground had slid across one

another into a new configuration. Now the shadow of her wings spanned either side of Faolan's elongated body. Gwynneth inhaled sharply.

A *flying wolf!* The sun went behind a cloud and the shadows vanished. But the image lingered in Gwynneth's mind's eye.

As she was contemplating it, she caught a disturbing sound in her ear slits. It was a tiny crackling coming from beneath the snowy surface deep in the earth.

Oh, no! she thought. *It can't be.* She had heard that sound before — a prelude to the last earthquake when she was in the Shadow Forest at the blue spruce. *Not again!* Should she alert the wolves below? She didn't want to alarm them unnecessarily. They were going at a fairly good clip. Banja had slowed down some. She was carrying Maudie, who was sound asleep in her jaws. Perhaps she could relieve her. Gwynneth swooped down. "Let me take the pup, Banja. You look tired."

"I'll do it," Edme offered. "Best you keep scouting, Gwynneth."

"Oh, you are both too kind," Banja said and shook her head slightly as if she could hardly believe this generosity. It was not the first time Banja had looked upon kindness with astonishment. Ever since she had joined them with her pup, she seemed overwhelmed when the wolves were nice to her. Why had she never been this way at the Ring? Did she have to give birth to learn that the world was not a stingy place?

The glare was exceptionally fierce as they headed into the setting sun. Faolan soon noticed that Banja was not the only one who had grown tired; the others' energy seemed to be flagging as well. He was determined to reach the border and the Cave Before Time by evening. He knew now that this was where he would meet the third *gyre*. There had been Eo, and before Eo, Fionula. Who would be the third?

He slid his eyes toward Edme, who was trotting beside him. She had handed off the pup to Mhairie. Sometimes he felt that Edme perceived more about him than he did himself. He wondered about the nightmare she'd had in the spirit woods. What had she seen as he had walked with his *gyre* souls? Did she sense who that third soul would be?

Impossible!

"You're thinking about the Cave, aren't you? The Cave Before Time," Edme asked.

"I'd — I'd just like to get there by dark." He tried to sound casual.

Edme said nothing. He noticed that her gait was rough. At first he thought it was because she had been carrying Maudie. But now he turned and looked as she walked a bit ahead of him. Her starboard leg was striking the ground unevenly.

"Edme, are you lame?"

Edme wheeled around. "What? No! I'm perfectly fine."

"You're walking as if you have a pain. Pain in your starboard femur."

Edme laid back her ears, barely disguising a snarl. "My femur is perfectly fine."

Her femur was not perfectly fine. Faolan knew it. He could feel that it was twisted. He wasn't sure why he had never noticed this before. Perhaps it hadn't affected her when she was younger. It could have been bone freeze, a condition that often afflicted elderly wolves. Gradually the bone twisted and became gnarled, which made for an uneven gait. But the condition never occurred in a wolf as young as Edme.

If it was bone freeze, it seemed grossly unfair to Faolan. Poor Edme! Because she was a *malcadh* made and not born, her eye had not been restored, and now a twisted femur that could not be detected at birth and probably had not troubled her until this long journey had flared up. Faolan could tell that Edme was angry, especially when he mentioned her femur. This all seemed oddly familiar to him. Her annoyance with him, the funny way she walked, her defensiveness when he said the word "femur." He had to think of something quickly to placate her.

"I'm sure it's nothing. We would all be walking a bit peculiarly if we had fallen into a crevasse and had to hang on to that ice ledge such a long time."

"Exactly!" she mumbled. "Now please drop the subject." She picked up her speed as if to prove she was fine.

Faolan watched her as she moved off. There was something haunting about the way she was walking, something that scratched at the back of his brain, like an old dream. *Dream!* That was it! He'd had a dream the night before the earthquake on Broken Talon Point.

While his sisters were carving the bones of their mother, Morag, he had fallen into a deep sleep in a den nearby and dreamed of carving another bone, a twisted femur.

He stopped in his tracks. But how could that be? He could not have carved Edme's femur. He hadn't even known it was twisted. She had never before betrayed a trace of lameness. Suddenly, Faolan was frightened of what he would find in the Cave Before Time. *I can't go there*, he thought. *I can't!* His legs refused to move.

"Faolan, what's wrong?" the Whistler asked.

"I . . . I think I need to rest. Right here. I think we should stop here for the night."

"What!" Edme roared. "Have you gone *cag mag*?" She raced toward him, her ears shoved forward, her tail raised, and her hackles bristling. Her single eye gleamed and seemed to pin him to the ground as Faolan sank down into the most abject posture of submission.

There was absolute silence. One could have heard a feather drop or a strand of fur shed. Never had the wolves seen Edme and Faolan face off in such a display. To see Faolan, of all wolves, sinking down as if he were once again a gnaw wolf, and Edme rigid, her ears shoved forward as if her marrow was about to boil over with anger . . . There had been many strange things that had occurred in the Beyond during the last moon, but this was the strangest of all.

All the creatures, the six wolves, the two pups, and the two bear cubs froze in their tracks. This standoff was a spectacle that not one of them could have anticipated. They all knew, even the young pups, that Faolan and Edme had a profound respect for each other. They had both been gnaw wolves in their clans. They had both competed in the *gaddergnaw* and earned themselves coveted positions on the Watch at the Ring. To see them fight was as peculiar as the unseasonable moons that had brought blizzards in the summer.

Faolan felt a shiver course up his paw right through the swirling marks on its pad. He saw Edme's hackles bristle up and a frightened light in her eye replaced the glint. Her tail dropped. At just that moment Gwynneth lighted down.

"What are you standing here for? We have to move. I think —" There was a shudder from deep inside the earth.

"We have to move now!" Gwynneth said. "This ground could crack. There's softer ground ahead — a bog."

"The Frost Forest! It's at the edge of the bog. And then the Cave — the Cave Before Time. We have to get there." Faolan's voice was firm and an urgent new energy streamed through him.

He raced forward. Edme and the rest of the little company fell in on his port flank. The earth was shaking, but the motley brigade of creatures raced on, confident that even if the land cracked, order had been restored for them. Faolan was in the lead, Edme beside him, then his sisters with Myrr between them, the cubs next. The Whistler carrying Maudie, and Banja at his side.

"Crevice opening to port!" Gwynneth shreed. The raspy call cut like a blade through the lavender twilight that was beginning to stain the land. Faolan headed a few points off course to skirt a gash that was opening up.

A minute later, Gwynneth sounded another alarm. "Press starboard now! There's another dead ahead!"

They were traveling at press-paw speed. "It's like a *byrrgis*," Mhairie whispered to Dearlea, "except we're the prey!" The ground fractured all around them, like a furious beast that would swallow them if they made the slightest misstep. Immense slashes opened up to the front of the wolves, behind them, and on all sides. The land was a deadly maze.

"Bear two points off to port, three! Now three to starboard! Quarter off the wind!" Edme had taken the lead and Faolan fell back. It was uncanny, but the one-eyed she-wolf seemed to sense the cracks before they opened. They ran on and on until the land finally stopped heaving.

Faolan shouted the order to halt. "We're here!" The creatures skidded to a stop. The ground was solid but ahead there was a tumble of rocks. The entrance to the Cave was blocked.

"Where are we?" Gwynneth asked, setting down on a large boulder.

"This is the Cave . . . the Cave Before Time." Faolan looked at Edme.

"Lead us in, Faolan," she said softly. "You know the way."

And he did. The swirl on the once twisted paw of his was drawn to an almost invisible passage, like a lodestone to a strong rock.

"This way!" Faolan said. "This way."

CHAPTER TWENTY-FIVE

"He Still Lives"

THE PATH INTO THE CAVE HAD altered. It twisted and turned, then pitched quite steeply. Faolan proceeded cautiously. He was sure this was the Cave Before Time, but the quake must have rearranged its interior as it had the rest of the world outside. He wondered what had happened to the beautiful pictures.

He stepped into a cavern, and though it was black as night, a filament of moonlight fell down upon him from above. *The moon crack!* Faolan thought. He had seen this crack before, so he now knew exactly where he was in the Cave. But how strange that the moon crack had remained just as it always was, no wider than before despite the two earthquakes.

On his first visit to the cave, Faolan had thought he was entering a cavern of impenetrable darkness, but there had been a tiny fissure in the ceiling no bigger then the thread of a spiderweb. And through it fell a silken strand of moonlight. For most creatures this would not provide enough light to see, but a wolf's night vision was truly extraordinary and the thin beam of moonlight offered just enough illumination. Now it caught the wolves' eyeshine, first from Faolan's eyes, and then those of the other wolves. Suddenly, the cave flickered with green light. The pictures loomed up on the mica-flecked walls, undamaged even in the latest convulsions of the earth. In a far corner, Faolan spied a mound of pure white fur. The mound stirred. The cave flashed as four eyes met in a lock of green shine.

"Airmead!" Edme yelped. "Katria!"

Airmead and Katria had belonged to the MacHeath clan, the only two noble wolves in a clan so heinous it had been expelled from the Beyond more than four hunger moons ago. Airmead had been the Obea of the clan and Katria the former mate of Donaidh, a high-ranking lieutenant. Before the clan's expulsion, both Airmead and Katria had escaped the MacHeaths to join the MacNamara clan, where they had proven themselves invaluable. They had been dispatched to serve on the Blood Watch by the MacNamara chief and arrived soon after Faolan and Edme had left.

The Whistler now stepped forward. "But the rest, the rest of the Blood Watch? Where are they?"

Katria and Airmead looked at each other and Airmead tried to stand. It was then they noticed the huge streak of blood on her flank.

"Down, Airmead!" Katria ordered. She turned to Faolan and Edme. "Airmead was wounded in a skirmish with the last rout."

"The last rout?" Faolan said. "You mean there are no more outclanner packs?"

"Just the remnants of one. Lupus knows where they went."

"There were twelve in the rout. Now there are perhaps five — six at the most. Vicious! You can't believe how vicious." Airmead shook her head. She winced and Edme noticed that there was blood leaking from her neck as well.

"Stay quiet, Airmead. Your wound is in a dangerous place."

"Don't worry. It was worse last night and it's getting better every day. I'm gaining strength. There is actually plenty to eat in this cave — mice, voles, even bats if you're desperate enough."

"What about Brygeen?" the Whistler asked.

"Brygeen and the Namara — they're both gone," Airmead whispered.

They all gasped. Airmead seemed to know what passed through the wolves' minds. It was unthinkable that Galana the Namara, the chieftain of the MacNamara clan, leader of the greatest fighting force in the Beyond, had been killed by a rout of outclanners.

"It wasn't the rout that killed the Namara," Katria replied. "She had arrived to help out on the Blood Watch just before the first quake. She had hardly been here a day when it happened." Katria closed her eyes and recalled the scene.

First came the terrible growling that rose up from the earth as if a maddened beast had been set loose. The Namara was thrown from the cairn on which she stood watch, flung out into the air to land on a jagged rock. The tip of the rock impaled her, piercing right through her chest and into her heart.

"What is it, Katria?" Edme asked as she saw the she-wolf's hackles had risen and her legs were shaking.

"She can't stand to think about it," Airmead whispered. "She is the one who saw the Namara's death. She didn't die at the fangs of the outclanners, but her death caused the skirmish in which I was injured and Brygeen and Alastrine were killed."

"Alastrine, too?" Mhairie moaned. Alastrine was the *skreeleen* and point wolf from the Blue Rock Pack of the MacDuncan clan. Both Mhairie and Dearlea revered her. There were very few she-wolves who had the lungs to run as fast as a point wolf needed to, and also serve as the *skreeleen*, the lead howler in a pack.

"I don't understand," Edme said. "How could the death of the Namara cause a battle between the Blood Watch and an outclanners' rout?"

"Heart's blood," Airmead said softly.

"What are you talking about?" Faolan asked.

"When the first earthquake came and the Namara was thrown from her cairn, she landed on a splinter of rock that pierced her heart. There's that stupid old superstition about the blood that comes from the heart of a chieftain. Some believe that if one drinks it, they become invincible. The Namara was the most powerful of all wolves. So the outclanners raced in to lap up her blood. It was an abomination! They were tearing at her pelt, going wild trying to devour her heart."

"But it's *cag mag*," Edme whispered. "She was powerful because she was intelligent, unlike any outclanner in any rout. She was of strong marrow. That same marrow that made her fight so well and inspired her as a leader also made her compassionate. So they tear out her heart, drink her heart's blood to make them strong? They don't even know what real strength is. Stupid, stupid superstitious wolves!"

Faolan cocked his head toward Edme. She sounded exactly like the Sark, who had nothing but contempt for the old wolf superstitions. How often had he heard the Sark carry on about the submission rituals or the silly necklaces that the chieftains wore? But at the same time, the speech was pure Edme. He recalled vividly how Edme had defended him at the *gaddergnaw* against the loathsome yellow wolf Heep when they were in a gnaw circle honing their bone-carving skills for the final contest. Faolan had gnawed a picture of a constellation that Heep had said was blasphemous, for it resembled the Great Bear constellation more than the Great Wolf one. The conversation came back to him as if it were yesterday.

It looks like a bear and not a wolf. Heep had scowled. But Edme had come to Faolan's defense. Her voice so soft but her words so incisive they cut like fangs to bone.

It's beautiful, Heep, she had said. *What difference does it make what one calls it? Stars all have different meaning for different animals, and heavens have different names.* Her words had been so simple and yet so powerful.

Then a terrible thought raced through Faolan's mind.

"Airmead, Katria, was there a yellow wolf in that rout?" Faolan asked suddenly.

"Why, yes. Yes, there was."

"Was he tailless?" Faolan asked. Edme turned to him quickly, horrified understanding in her eyes.

"But, Faolan, Heep was a *malcadh* — a true *malcadh*. He would have been mended."

"True," Faolan said.

How unfair. Here is Edme still with just one eye, and Heep's tail has been restored. He turned again to Katria and Airmead. "It is also true that this yellow wolf was a murderer. He murdered a *malcadh*!"

"What?" the two wolves gasped.

"Yes, and he was a MacDuncan wolf, not a MacHeath. Tell me, was he one of the ones who survived? Does Heep still live?"

Airmead and Katria both nodded. "He was the one who wounded me, Faolan. Of course it was Heep! I should have remembered him, but with his tail he looked so different. But yes, Faolan, he still lives."

CHAPTER TWENTY-SIX

THE MOON CRACK

HE STILL LIVES. THE WORDS ECHOED in Faolan's mind, shivered through his marrow. The wolves had all settled down in the spacious first *heal*, or chamber, of the Cave. Although Faolan was exhausted, he knew sleep would not come easily. He looked up at the moon crack.

Faolan realized that he had become so distracted by the story of Heep and the outclanners' greed for heart's blood, that he had completely forgotten about the third *gyre* of his soul — his brethren through time, through the centuries. He needed Fionula, the Snowy Owl, and Eo, the grizzly, and whomever the third *gyre* creature was, if he was going to attempt to leave the Beyond and find a new land to the west. The Distant Blue, past the farthest edges of the outclanners' territory, where the western sea began.

The Distant Blue loomed azure and cloudless like another sky. It had always been unreachable because of that western sea that was too vast to swim, but through his *gyres*, Faolan sensed that there might be a way. Was this not how the first wolves of the Beyond had arrived out of the Long Cold on the Ice March?

It came to him then as he thought about the Distant Blue that his third soul was a wolf. He was not sure how he knew this, but the knowledge struck him with such conviction that it was impossible to doubt.

He was sure his wolf *gyre* soul was needed to lead them out of the Beyond to this new place, the Distant Blue. And of course it wasn't a truly new place. It was the place from which they had all come — the place the wolves had left when they had arrived in the Beyond on the Ice March, more than a thousand years ago. Once there had been a wolf, an old wolf, who had led them. Faolan must meet that wolf tonight, right now while his companions slept.

He looked over at Edme before he stood up. She was lovely in her sleep, lovely in her bones. It was as if that shimmering spirit of hers shone through from her marrow to her pelt. She was the best of all things a wolf could be, a container for all grace. Despite her missing eye, she was a wolf so lovely in her marrow that she made the rest of the world seem dim and shadowed by comparison.

Faolan raised up onto his legs. They felt slightly wobbly, as if he were much older and weaker than his age. He limped off to follow the moon crack. He knew it ran all through the winding tunnels and *heals* of the Cave, this Cave Before Time. And he knew that when he came to the end of the last passage, he would meet his final *gyre* soul — the frost wolf.

As he walked, Faolan felt his two other *gyre* souls fall in on either side of him and thought what fine company they were. Though they didn't speak a word, there was a kind of communion between them that made talking unnecessary. They would pause to gaze at the drawings in the flickering thread of the moon's silvery light. Here and there, Faolan spotted a swirl of spiraling lines, just like the marks on his paw. But it was the other drawings that fascinated him the most. The rock seemed to breathe with the panting of animals and the stamp of their footsteps. Their wing beats made gusty sounds that echoed from the stone walls. Faolan stopped in front of what had always been his favorite picture in the Cave — a flowing line of wolves on the hunt. He had been mesmerized by the image as a yearling. He had not known then that a hunting formation was called a *byrrgis*. At the time, all he wanted was to join in that flowing line of wolves, to belong, to be a part of something larger than himself.

And now a truth broke upon him as he stood closer. The point wolf in the painting! His stride was so familiar. *I know a wolf who runs like that!* He inhaled sharply as recognition exploded in his head. *I am that wolf!* He blinked. It was as if he were standing with one paw in the now and another in the before, where he was leading a *byrrgis*. He could hear the pounding of the feet of hundreds upon hundreds of wolves behind him. He was the leader. This was the third *gyre*! Beneath the drawing was the spiraling mark from his paw. It had been placed with a deliberation, unlike the others which had been randomly scattered throughout the cave. He realized what that placement in this particular spot meant. It was his signature, his sign. He had been the one to make this drawing!

Faolan continued down a winding, sloping incline and came to another drawing with bold marks made by a black rock. He recognized it immediately. *Ah, yes,* he thought. The picture showed the first night he had seen an outclanner come feed on a wolf who had collapsed into unconsciousness from famine. The spirit of Eo, the grizzly *gyre* soul, had risen within Faolan and struck the outclanner dead with one blow of his paw. Beneath the drawing was a bear claw, the swirling marks on its pad. He felt the thunderous heart of the grizzly rumbling within his own chest.

Faolan squeezed through the narrow passageways and channels of the Cave that opened on to new *heals* with drawings he had never before seen, all rendered by his *gyre* souls, some with the mark of the bear claw, some with Fionula's mark, the claws of her talons twisting into a swirl. But it was the oldest pictures, the ones made by the wolf, that were the most mysterious to him and somehow the most familiar. He stopped in front of one that depicted a wolf on a well-known ridge near the ring of Sacred Volcanoes. It showed a wolf whom he knew to be a Fengo in an intimate conversation with an owl — a Spotted Owl that must have been a collier, for a bucket of embers rested next to him. Faolan had dreamed about just this scene half a moon before, on the night that he had slept at the cairn of the Fengos. It was Grank the first collier, and the first Fengo. They had been best friends.

A light breeze seemed to stir Fionula's feathers, as if to confirm the answer to the question. The *gyres* moved through a narrow passageway where there was barely a trickle of moonlight. *To what depths does the cave plunge?* Faolan was not sure which of his *gyres* asked the question, but they all moved forward. There was still the last *gyre* to meet and it was waiting — waiting for them.

They passed into a very small *heal*. Faolan stared at the wall ahead, which was covered by the most beautiful of all the drawings in the Cave. The wall curved as if it were made for just this story. *But it cannot be!* Faolan thought. *No! No one would dare make a picture of the moment of death, the moment of separation from clan, from pack, from one's own body. The sacred act of* cleave hwyln!

And yet the picture showed a wolf lying on the ground, so limp that he seemed almost boneless. His pelt looked like a discarded piece of fur. A starry ladder hung down from the Great Wolf constellation and the dim figure of an ancient wolf, a chieftain, was climbing up with the help of Skaarsgard, the Star Wolf guide to the Cave of Souls. The old wolf was clinging to the ladder as if he could barely hang on — or as if he didn't want to leave his pelt behind.

Faolan began to shiver and he felt the air beside him turn tremulous with the shuddering *gyre* souls of Eo and

Fionula. *The third* gyre *awaits us.* The words quivered in the air. The thread of light through the moon crack brightened, illuminating the base of the wall. Faolan gasped as his eyes fell upon a bone — the loveliest of bones polished by a thousand years or more of time. It was a femur, a twisted femur.

CHAPTER TWENTY-SEVEN

THE LOVELIEST
OF BONES

IN A SPIKE OF MOONLIGHT THE twisted femur beckoned Faolan. He walked forward, yet his own legs felt boneless. His heart hammered and the pounding of Eo's heart nearly deafened him. Fionula had *wilfed* until she was thinner than a filament of moonlight. The carving on the bone was more beautiful than any Faolan had ever seen. It began to tell a story, but Faolan knew instinctively that unless he picked up this bone, the story would never be complete, nor would he have the courage to continue through the stone passage following the curved wall. *I am about to meet the frost wolf.* And yet something seemed slightly wrong with those words — "frost wolf." He picked up the bone and crept close to the wall to follow its curve.

It was a continuation of the story of *cleave hwlyn*, but

where it would end he was unsure. He had heard this story before, when he was just a yearling, on a stormy night streaked with lightning. A *skreeleen* had begun to howl the tale of a dying chieftain from the time of the Long Cold. Slipping his pelt, his bones lying silent and cold in the moon's pale light, the chieftain had begun to climb the star ladder to the Cave of Souls.

The next picture on the wall showed a silent howl and a look of complete confusion on Skaarsgard's face as the old chieftain began falling, falling, his paws scratching the air as he tried to grab the rungs of the star ladder. And there the story appeared to end. But in a sense, the story was simply beginning anew, for now Faolan understood that the chieftain was reborn as the first Fengo, the wolf who led them out of the Long Cold and into the Beyond.

Around the final bend of the wall, Faolan would meet the third *gyre*. He clenched the femur tighter in his jaws, feeling the carvings on that lovely bone caress his tongue. There was something familiar about the lines in his mouth. *This is a story older than time*, they seemed to say. *Written in bone, a story of a journey and a love lost, a spirit forgotten and then met again and again. Your story, your story, all of your stories. Wolf, owl, bear, and wolf again. Now and forever.*

Faolan felt himself growing older, his heart slowing. *Cleave hwlyn* awaited him, but there was no turning back now. He was too curious. He must meet the last of his *gyres* and the first of his souls.

The moon crack suddenly widened into an immense aperture. White light poured through it and ahead a glistening figure appeared. It spoke and yet the voice seemed to be Faolan's own, to come from within his own throat.

Faolan felt as if he were looking in a mirror and the mirror image spoke back to him with his words, his voice. His body began to merge with another being much older than himself.

"I am Fengo! Fengo is my name and always has been. I am the Fengo of Fengos — the first Fengo!"

The frost wolf was unsure how long he had stood beneath the cataract of moonlight that poured down upon him. But something strange had begun to happen, as if time were curling back on itself. The light slid from black, to the glare of day, to First Lavender, followed by the Deep Purple before First Black. It was as if the frost wolf were accustoming himself to an old pelt he had forgotten. *I'll get used to it*, he told himself. *I'll gain strength, too.* For he knew he had done it before and would do it again.

He felt the *gyres* gather around him and press closely. The feathery touch of Fionula grazed his withers. The thunderous pumping from Eo's chest wrapped him in a cocoon as Faolan had once been wrapped up in the rhythms of his second Milk Giver's heart. Faolan felt the spirit of the frost wolf press in upon him, as did Fionula's and that of Eo. Three spirits to guide him to the Distant Blue.

There was no mystery now as to why he had been granted these extra lives, these *gyres* of his soul. It was his due as well as his choice. Once, he had slipped off the star ladder, picked up his pelt, and gone on to save the clans and lead them on the Ice March out of the Long Cold to somewhere safe for them. He had picked up the spirits of animals he had come to know or to admire — not only their souls, but their kind. He had been Fionula, a Snowy Owl, with the lovely voice of a gadfeather, and Eo, the largest of all the animals in the Beyond. And finally he once again became a wolf — a wolf named Faolan.

He had been blessed as no other creature on earth. He had felt the marrow of a wolf, the gizzard of an owl, and the heart of a grizzly. The frost wolf who was Fengo closed his eyes and saw all that he had been. He saw the *gyres* of his soul coming and going through the centuries that stretched over a millenium. And now it was time for farewell as the darkness dropped and the beginning of First Lavender settled a light mist in the air. Wind shadows shuddered through the *heal*. It was time to move out of this stony place. For Faolan to move on with the spirits of Fengo the frost wolf, Fionula the Snowy Owl, and Eo the grizzly at his side.

CHAPTER TWENTY-EIGHT

"WHO IS THIS?"

"FAOLAN?" MYRRGLOSCH SAID IN a tiny voice and blinked up at the silver wolf. Faolan looked larger and brighter than before, his luminous pelt glistening like ice. He had never seemed more powerful.

The other wolves were startled as well. They knew the wolf before them was Faolan, but he had changed in some inexplicable way. Edme took a step forward, and began to tremble as she saw the bone near Faolan's paws. She sensed in Faolan a spirit that seemed to shine through him. Something familiar that had been lost to her through the millenium. There was a tingling of excitement in her marrow, the feeling of old souls reunited.

Faolan felt Edme's eye pierce through the ghosts of his many hearts, of the marrow and gizzard of all the creatures he had been. *She sees what she cannot quite understand,* he thought.

A word bloomed in Edme's head like an ice flower. *Fengo!* Fengo was what she had always called him — not the title of Fengo, but simply Fengo, for that had been her mate's name.

A calm had stolen into the *heal*. "It's time for us to go now," Faolan said. In his head he heard Fionula. *You must leave immediately. Leave now when the Deep Purple hinges on the First Black of night.*

It was a fair jump out from the Cave and through the wide opening of the moon crack. Myrr scrambled onto Faolan's back. Gwynneth gently took Maudie in her talons, but just before Edme was about to make her jump, Faolan called down to her. "Bring the bone, dear. It's time we returned it."

CHAPTER TWENTY-NINE

THE CRYSTAL PLAIN

AFTER LEAVING THE CAVE BEFORE Time, the animals spent nearly half a moon before they emerged on a high plain of sparkling snow. Under the dome of a star-scattered night it seemed as if millions of the stars had fallen about them into the snow. They felt engulfed in a tumult of starlight and began to nervously scratch the ground.

"Is this a frozen sea, the western sea?" the Whistler asked.

"No," Faolan replied. "We still have a fair trek to the western sea."

"A glacier — is this what we are on?" Banja asked fearfully, pulling her pup close to her.

"No." Faolan planted his forepaw firmly in the snow and lifted it, making a mark of shimmering swirled lines, like a comet come to earth. "This is the Crystal Plain. Each flake of snow is so dry that it is a perfect prism for the light. During the day it will be too bright to travel across so we must make our way by night, or else be blinded like Beezar, the stumbling wolf of the night sky. So let us begin now and at dawn we'll stop and dig in. It will take us several days to cross the plain, but we must never travel in daylight. It is simply too dangerous."

A question hung in everyone's minds, but they dared not utter it. How would they ever cross the western sea? If they could not cross the sea, how would they ever reach the Distant Blue?

They had just taken their first steps onto the Crystal Plain. It was windless and an astonishing silence fell on the world. A blanket of stars billowed in the darkness and the creatures felt themselves wrapped in the pelt of the night. Suddenly, their hackles bristled and they each tipped their head up as mist swept down onto the high plain. From the youngest to the oldest, they all sensed that spirits moved among them.

Narrowing their eyes until they were slits of green, amber, or coal black, they spied the familiars of their hearts and gizzards and marrows. There was the Namara, and beside her Oona and then Brygeen. Katria and

Airmead began the howling known as *glaffling*, the howls of mourning. Gwynneth pressed her wings above her head and she bowed down midair to the scroom of King Soren in the owl gesture of mourning known as Glaux griven. "Mum!" The two cubs reached out into the spangled night to touch the *lochin* of their mother, Bronka. The feathers fixed in their withers quivered. Edme threw back her head, jewel-like tears weeping from her eye as she glimpsed her old *taiga*, Winks.

The gathering of *lochin* sparkled in the night so brightly that it made the Crystal Plain seem dim in comparison. And soon there came a starry wolf with the powerful shoulders of an outflanker. Beside her strode a huge grizzly. They were creatures so different, yet they shared a precious bond. Both had offered their milk to sustain a pup, a *malcadh* who grew up strong, a *malcadh* who would lead the living out of the Beyond.

"Mum! Thunderheart!" Faolan exclaimed. Mhairie and Dearlea pressed close to Faolan and together they sunk down on their knees for this last good-bye.

But where is the Sark? Gwynneth swiveled her head, flipped it forward then back and swiveled it again. *Oh, Sark, where are you?* And then she recalled the Sark did not believe in *lochin* or scrooms. "Stuff and nonsense" she had called them more than once. The Masked Owl wept as if her heart were broken.

As quickly as the spirits had come, they melted into the blackness of the night and were gone. The eight wolves, the two pups, the cubs, and the owl began their journey again in complete silence, for this was the end of the world as they knew it.

The Beyond was behind them. Ahead was the Distant Blue.

An hour before dawn, as the last evening star, known as Hilgeen, began to slip down in the dome of the night and the blackness shredded to gray, Faolan called a halt. "We must stop now. Soon the sun will come up and we must not see it!"

"But there are no caves here, no dens," the Whistler said, looking about.

"We must build one."

"Build?" Airmead asked and all the wolves looked at one another in complete bewilderment. Even the word "build" was an unfamiliar one to them. Birds built nests, but wolves — what could wolves build?

"I'll show you, and you shall soon be experts, I promise you."

Faolan began digging furiously with his paws. Snow flew up into the air, landing behind him. Soon there was a small pile. "Come on now, you see how I've done it. Start digging. Make sure all the snow goes into that pile."

"How much snow do we need?" Mhairie asked. Faolan stopped. He looked at the two bear cubs. "Stand up tall, Toby and Burney." He looked at them. "The pile should be as tall as the withers on the cubs. For we must all fit in."

When they had amassed a big enough pile of snow, Faolan said, "Now we must pack it tightly. Cubs, your paws are the broadest. So begin to press the snow so it is firm. We shall help you. And, Gwynneth, your wings should be useful in patting the snow down so the walls are firm."

It did not take long. Faolan tested the mound. "The snow must bind before we make a tunnel."

"A tunnel?" Myrr asked.

"Yes, of course. We have to hollow out the mound so there is room for us."

When the snow firmed, Faolan began the tunnel. "Myrrglosch and Maudie, you can help. This is where we need little wolves to squeeze in alongside me to make the opening wider."

By dawn the snow cave was complete. It was a peculiar structure like none they had ever slept in before, but it was snug. It protected them against the wind and most important, against the glare of the sun.

The creatures soon became proficient in building the curious domed caves. Toby and Burney became skillful snow packers and Myrr and Maudie were excellent at squeezing in on either side of whoever was the "tunneler." Gwynneth, too, with her long, sharp talons, became an excellent excavator.

"And to think," she said one dawn as she furiously flung back talonfuls of snow, "that burrowing owls used to be the only ones trusted with digging. What would they say if they saw me now!"

All day, the companions slept in the snow caves and then, when the sun dropped down below the horizon, they crawled out and began their nightly trek across the Crystal Plain. Faolan took the lead, leaving his clear swirling print in the sparkling snow.

Edme, who had known Faolan better than any of the other wolves, felt a myriad of sometimes confusing feelings and emotions as they traveled farther and farther west. She sensed spirits that seemed to stir in the radiance that emanated from Faolan. And the bone that she carried with her both troubled and comforted her. The incisions in it were beautiful, but she could barely understand them. They were incised in Old Wolf, a language of which she only knew a few expressions that had lingered on among the wolves. However, she sensed that it was part of a very old story that had been left untold. Edme slid her eyes toward Faolan as she trotted alongside him. He often blurted out Old Wolf phrases, phrases that no wolf of their time should have known.

Although the mysterious pain in her hind leg still troubled her, Edme was walking better. She sensed the pain was connected with the bone she carried. *If I set it down, would I begin to limp again?* she wondered.

They were nearly across the Crystal Plain. The snow became coarser as they approached the western sea, and building the snow caves was trickier.

One evening, soon after they had left what was to be their last snow cave, Gwynneth was flying above the somewhat straggling line of creatures. Banja was carrying her own pup and helping Myrr along as well, entertaining him with some of the lively shanties that the Watch wolves used to sing when the She-Winds blew and all the colliers and Rogue smiths would come to collect bonk coals from the surge of erupting volcanoes. For some reason, these old shanties made Gwynneth think of her earliest days in the Beyond, when she had first come there with her father, Gwyndor, and met the Sark.

The Sark! How Gwynneth missed her and with each league away from the Beyond and toward the Distant Blue, the more keen the feeling. If the Sark could have only held on, perhaps they could have gotten her well enough for this journey. *If only . . .* Gwynneth supposed that life was filled with regrets and if onlys.

More than once, Gwynneth's auntie had said that the world is not fair. Certainly it had not been fair that the MacHeath clan had tried to start a war between the wolves and the bears. It wasn't fair that Edme was a *malcadh* made and not born. If fairness were the rule, the good would not die young, as Coryn, the king of the Great Tree, had. The vicious and the depraved would be immediately swept away to the eternal flames of the Dim World.

The world was not fair. However, on this cloudless night of crisp, clear air high above the Crystal Plain, it was beautiful. And Gwynneth, who could travel so much faster than the wolves, decided to take a moment to trace a constellation. This was how all young owlets learned to navigate, by tracing the season's constellations. She did a banking turn and flew off toward the east — the hatching sky as the owls called it. This was where the constellations were born each night, just as the Deep Purple began to settle and the stars began to rise. Like chicks clambering over the edge of a nest to explore what was out there, like wolf pups impatient to see the white light at the opening of a whelping den, stars, too, scrambled over the rim of the new night to take their place in the big world.

"Ah!" Gwynneth exclaimed as she saw the first claw of the Little Raccoon. "But, Beezar!" she said suddenly. "Beezar, what are you doing here?" She addressed the first stars of the constellation as if they could hear her.

Gwynneth realized they were Beyond the Beyond, beyond the Outermost. She was the farthest west she had ever been, and the farthest south. And now the poor staggering blind wolf Beezar had left the Beyond and was following them toward the Distant Blue.

New land, new territory! the Masked Owl thought. *But the things we leave behind!*

The thought was as sharp as a blade hot from the forge. She could not help but think of the Sark, her bones now mingled with the shards of pottery on the floor of her cave.

At just that moment, Gwynneth spied the top of a new constellation that seemed to be clawing its way over the dark edge of the eastern night in a most determined manner.

What could that be? she wondered. It looked vaguely familiar, but she was sure she had never seen it before.

CHAPTER THIRTY

A WOLF NAMED ALIAC

"JUST FOLLOW THE TIP!" HEEP called out and flicked his tail.

"This is the first sensible thing he has ever done with that *loc na mhuice* thing," Heep's mate, Aliac, muttered.

"Ma, did you curse?" Abban said.

Aliac turned around in the dark tunnel of this strange cave and blinked at her little son. "Why do you call me "Ma"? That's not a proper name."

"What do you mean?" Abban asked. "Every wolf calls their ma . . . Ma. What other word is there?"

"Mum," she said and blinked again. Where in the world had that come from? The word seemed familiar, but she couldn't quite place it. "Call me Mum, but perhaps not around your father. And, yes, I did curse." She paused. "Don't be like me!"

She felt a shudder pass through her. *Because I really don't know who I am.* "Come along now. We have to follow the others. Your father has hopes of us getting out of here."

"You mean this cave?"

"I mean this whole terrible place of endless winter and no food and earthquakes and Lupus knows what else."

"Pa liked the earthquake. It gave him his tail back."

"Yes, so I've noticed."

There was a sneer in her voice that Abban had never before heard. But he trotted along, looking around the rumps of the other wolves for the flickering tail his father raised so proudly. They were traveling through a beautiful cave with strange drawings on the walls. Abban had never seen anything like it before.

Heep had picked up a familiar scent early on in the cave. There had been a mixture of scents from other wolves and possibly bears, but he had teased out an old familiar smell. What would Faolan do when he saw Heep with a tail? And not only with a tail, but with a handsome mate and a son! His old adversary, the very wolf who had caused him to be chased from the Beyond, what would he say or do now?

Faolan was clever, smart. Heep knew that if anyone could find his way to another place, it was the splay-pawed wolf. He supposed that Faolan had also been mended now, his paw turned right and that distinct print with the spiraling marks erased. Faolan had learned how to walk in a way that disguised his track, but he couldn't disguise his scent and Heep would follow it.

Heep stopped. Faolan's scent began to grow dimmer as he rounded a long curved wall. At the end, it simply vanished and there was a new unfamiliar scent, mingled with the older ones of the other wolves and the bear cubs. He caught sight of a feather blowing through the darkness.

"What's this?" he said.

At that moment Aliac came up to him. "It's a feather."

"Of course it's a feather," he snarled.

She rolled her eyes at him. "It's an owl feather, a Masked Owl, if I'm not mistaken."

Heep shoved his ears forward and bared his teeth, lifting his tail straight out. "Tuck it, Aliac! Tuck it!" She quickly folded her tail between her legs in a gesture of submission. Heep relaxed. "We'll continue now."

He tried to maintain his confident stride, but he was nervous. This new scent made him uneasy.

Soon the rout came to a *heal* where there was a large opening to the sky. They tipped their heads up and saw rafts of stars scudding by.

"Look at this!" Abban said.

"What?" his father snapped.

"This print — a swirling star!"

Heep felt his blood run cold as he looked down at the paw print.

"But there's no scent!" he roared. "No scent!"

"What are you talking about?" Aliac said. "I smell the scent of at least five wolves, one nursing pup, and some bear cubs."

Heep lunged at Aliac and struck her above the eye with his claws.

But Aliac did not sink into the expected postures of submission.

"Down! Tail tuck!" Heep growled.

"Strike me again like that, you fool, and you will have no tail to tuck or wave. I shall tear it from your bony old rump!"

"Aliac!" The yellow wolf Heep was stunned. "You wouldn't dare."

"Oh, yes, I would. I can lead this rout as well as anyone," she turned to the others and glared. Rags was the first to sink into a posture of submission. Then Fynoff and Bevan. "I was a turning guard. One of the best. I can press a *byrrgis* at attack speed and reverse them in the blink of an eye if a bull moose goes rogue in a run."

"Aliac!"

"Don't call me that. It's not my name!"

A vague look came into the she-wolf's eyes. There was such stillness in the *heal*. A long, palpable quietness like grains of silence falling through the moon crack above began to fill the space. Abban spotted a glimmer in the deep green of his mother's eyes. He nestled close to her forepaws.

"My name is Caila. Caila, turning guard of the Carreg Gaer *byrrgis* of the MacDuncan clan. Mother of Mhairie and Dearlea and Abban." *And I have lost during the famine every pup I once had save for this one. And, by Lupus, I won't lose Abban.*

The next thing Abban knew, he was in the firm grip of his mother's jaws and seemed to be flying through the air and into the starry night.

She had picked him up again in her jaws and streaked off across the dazzling plain of snow, away from the vicious rout and the half life she had been living.

CHAPTER THIRTY-ONE

CAILA!

GWYNNETH WAS MOMENTARILY distracted from the curious constellation rising in the sky by a streak to the east. At first she thought it was a falling star low on the horizon. But then she realized that it was a creature — a body running stretched out, running as if . . .

Gwynneth's mind stopped, but her wings did not. *Running like a turning guard! Caila!* The name exploded in Gwynneth's head. She carved a steep banking turn and began to plunge.

Great Glaux, she's running with a pup in her jaws!

"Caila!" Gwynneth screeched.

The wolf hardly broke stride.

"Caila!" Gwynneth shreed this time, emitting a piercing shriek as she dived straight down. Caila had to swerve to avoid her, and skidded to a halt.

"Gwynneth!" She softly dropped the pup in her jaws. "What are you doing here?"

"I might ask the same of you! Everyone thinks you're dead. Mhairie, Dearlea."

"Mhairie, Dearlea." She said their names so softly as if she were caressing them. "My daughters."

Gwynneth regarded her gravely. "You denied them."

"I what?"

It all came back to Caila. The terrible night when out of nowhere Mhairie and Dearlea appeared, her two second milk daughters. She had raised them and they had never known that she was not their first Milk Giver. One never revealed such things. Except on that night, her brain muddled, she had told them, and not only that, but denied them. The horrendous words she had spoken rang now in her head: *I was never your mother. I deny you, I deny you, I deny you!*

This was the curse of a faithful mate to an unfaithful partner but was never uttered to children. And yet she had done just that, done the unthinkable. Seconds later, an outclanner had attacked her and shortly after, Heep had found her, staggering about, bleeding and in a daze. For Heep she was an experiment of sorts. Could a clan wolf be turned, be made useful to his rout? He thought he had accomplished it, until the moment she had regained her senses in the long winding tunnel of the Cave Before Time.

She shook her head now in disgust and disbelief. "How could I deny my own daughters?" Could they ever forgive her? she wondered. It was probably too late.

She looked up at Gwynneth, her muzzle trembling. "Are Mhairie and Dearlea dead now? Did they die in the famine?"

"No, no, not at all. They are not too far ahead of you. But how did you get here? Across the Crystal Plain?"

"I ran, ran like I never have before."

"In the day?"

"Never! I found snow caves."

"The ones we dug."

Caila blinked. "I thought there was a familiar scent in those snow caves. It had to be that of Dearlea and Mhairie. A Milk Giver never really forgets, except — I did, didn't I? For a long while." Her eyes welled with tears.

"Don't cry. They are not far away. I can lead you to them."

"Who are Mhairie and Dearlea?" Abban asked.

Caila leaned down to lick her pup. "Your sisters! And we are going to meet them!"

"I'll carry your pup," Gwynneth said. "You'll be able to run faster. Just follow me. We have to get to them before morning."

CHAPTER THIRTY-TWO

THE LAST DEN

THE COMPANIONS' LAST SHELTER wasn't a snow cave, but the kind of shelter they might have found in the Beyond. So they called it the Last Den. It was more of a cliff's overhang than a proper den, and it was at the edge of the western sea. Far behind them on the Crystal Plain, a new day was breaking, but they were safe from the glare. Ahead of them, like a glistening bow, a bridge of ice arced across the sea toward the Distant Blue.

Gwynneth alighted on the crescent of beach.

"You're here at last," Edme said. "We were beginning to worry."

"What happened?" Faolan asked as he stepped forward and his paw made the distinctive print in the sand. He fell back in surprise as he took in the pup she carried.

"I've found someone."

Caila stepped out from behind a beach boulder, her head down, her tail between her legs, her ears laid flat. Mhairie and Dearlea looked at each other and began to tremble. The little pup came up to them.

"Mum says you are my sisters. I've never had sisters."

Caila raised her head. "He wants to be your brother and I want to be your mum. I so, so want to be your mum again. I am so sorry." She crumpled to her knees in front of Mhairie and Dearlea.

They both put their muzzles close to her head and began to lick her ears, her nose. First one then the other ever so gently took her muzzle in their jaws. These were the gestures of forgiveness, of absolution.

"You gave us milk," Dearlea said.

"You loved us as well as our first Milk Giver," Mhairie said.

"You taught us to run in *byrrgises*. Mhairie became an outflanker."

"And Dearlea is a *skreeleen*."

Faolan stepped forward. "They never forgot you."

"But I forgot myself," she sobbed. "I forgot who I was, who I had been. My world turned inside out, upside down, and backward. Even my name . . ." She blinked. "It was backward. I was Aliac."

"But now you're Caila again," Faolan said.

"Yes, call me Caila," she said softly, and rolled her shoulders as if she were pleased to be back in her old pelt again.

Gwynneth launched into the purpling night and gave a joyous hoot.

"Look! Look to the sky."

A beautiful constellation of at least a dozen stars was rising over the Crystal Plain in the last of the night.

"I've never seen that one before," Edme said. "What should we call it?"

"The Sark!" Faolan exclaimed. "Look, it's a jug of stars! A memory jug!"

And for just a second it was as if he could see right through to the memories in that jug.

"Yes," Gwynneth said softly.

"Yes," Edme echoed. She tipped her head up, feeling as if her own story was just about to begin. She looked down at the twisted femur she had carried across the Crystal Plain, knowing it carried a love lost and a journey.

She looked out across the silvery bow of the ice

bridge. Tomorrow their true journey would begin. Nine wolves, three pups, an owl, and two bear cubs would step onto that bridge to cross the western sea to the Distant Blue and a new world.

A new beginning at the end of an old world.

AUTHOR'S NOTE

I WISH TO ACKNOWLEDGE MY debt to one of my favorite poets, W. B. Yeats. His two poems "The Second Coming" and "Sailing to Byzantium" were a particularly strong influence in writing *Spirit Wolf*. The phrase "no country for old wolves" was adapted for my wolf world directly from Yeats's poem "Sailing to Byzantium," in which the poet refers to the country of Ireland that the figure in the poem has left, as "no country for old men." The notion of the gyre, a conical shape, frequently appears throughout Yeats's poetry and is part of his complex philosophical system. He wrote about this philosophy in a book called *A Vision*. It was something that has intrigued me for years, ever since I first studied Yeats in college. I took this idea and adapted it for the notion of gyre souls. While gyre souls in truth bear no resemblance to Yeats's theory, nevertheless I am indebted to this great Irish poet whose words have continued to haunt me in the very best of ways for over forty years.